OREGON TRAIL: HELL ON WHEELS

By
JULIETTE DOUGLAS

COPYRIGHT

This is a remastered edition of
a previous Juliette Douglas title.

TABLE OF CONTENTS

COPYRIGHT

ACKNOWLEDGMENTS

FOREWARD

CHAPTER 1

CHAPTER 2

CHAPTER 3

CHAPTER 4

CHAPTER 5

CHAPTER 6

CHAPTER 7

CHAPTER 8

CHAPTER 9

CHAPTER 10

CHAPTER 11

CHAPTER 12

CHAPTER 13

CHAPTER 14

CHAPTER 15

CHAPTER 16

CHAPTER 17

CHAPTER 18

CHAPTER 19

CHAPTER 20

CHAPTER 21

CHAPTER 22

CHAPTER 23

CHAPTER 24

ABOUT THE AUTHOR

THE DOUGLAS COLLECTION

ACCLAIM FOR DOUGLAS

SNEAK PEEK

Miss Birgit's Dilemma

Chapter One

Chapter Two

Chapter Three

King

Prologue

Chapter 1

Chapter 2

Juliette Douglas

ACKNOWLEDGMENTS

Praise God for allowing me to see another sun. I am so thankful!

To that end, I want to thank my crafting buddies — Julie Clark Webber and Dianne Kraay — for being there for me. Bless you ladies!

FOREWORD

■ **By GERALD L. GUY**

The Oregon Trail was a grueling 2,000-mile route that led from Independence, Missouri to Oregon City, Oregon in 19th century America. Hundreds of thousands of pioneers, many with all they owned packed in wagons, drawn by horse and oxen, braved the rugged journey that snaked through present-day Missouri, Kansas, Nebraska, Wyoming and Idaho before reaching their destination. All coveted the rich promise of a new beginning in the unsettled West.

Marauding Indians, horrendous weather conditions, rugged mountain passes, rampaging rivers, isolation and sickness hampered the travelers. Thousands succumbed to the elements long before the end of the journey, which could span six or nine months. Historians estimate one in ten did not survive.

The trials did not end for those who made it to their destination. The West was wild, untamed country that required challenging work and determination in order to begin anew.

Authors have long romanticized the Oregon Trail because of its historic significance cannot be ignored. This is one of those stories.

(Hell on Wheels is a remastered edition of one of Juliette Douglas' earlier works.)

"Seeing America slowly was, in a way, like eating slow food. I wasn't covering much ground in a single day, but I was digesting a lot more."

RINKER BUCK, Author,
The Oregon Trail: A New American Journey

Juliette Douglas

CHAPTER 1

Late Spring 1850

Rifle shots splintered the air, the sound ricocheting off granite peaks. Startled, four men immediately halted their mounts. Ears perked up, and they listened hard.

James Lavanier spit a stream of brown juice before he said, "Sounds close."

Johan Svenson and Micah Cunningham nodded.

Packy Woods squinted and added, "Seams it's a-comin' from Sinking Springs."

Another volley of shots blistered the stillness, snapping the four men's attention.

Instinctively, they dug their heels into their mount's ribs and raced down the steep slope, still covered with melting winter snow. Their laden pack mules protested the pace.

Nearing the trading post, the four men disappeared into thick aspen and spruce cover.

Slipping from the leather, they grabbed their Hawken rifles and inched forward through the undergrowth.

Blood curdling yips reached their ears as they hunkered down behind deadfall and surveyed the chaos emanating around Trader Charley's store.

In desperate defense, spits of fire erupted from a lone rifle, each time moving to a different port.

Several bodies littered the packed earth.

Painted ponies wandered aimlessly.

Four sets of eyes focused on the rampaging marauders.

"Damn!" began Packy. "What's them sorry cayuses doing attacking Charley?"

Svenson's Swedish lilt carried his disgust. "Blackfeet," he spat.

"Them redskins is way outta their territory," voiced Lavanier. "That ain't no huntin' party neither," he added, spitting a stream of juice.

Micah looked at his compatriots and grinned, "Well, boys? We just gonna sit here and yap? What say ya we go help Charley?"

"Ya!" Svenson remarked. "I need a good cobweb cleaning."

Lavanier spit the well-worn chaw out of his mouth, and said, "Let 'er rip!" He jammed the Hawken to his shoulder. Quickly, he leveled it, picked a target and pulled the trigger.

Gunfire, in rapid succession, echoed against the hills of the deep hollow as the men reloaded and kept up the barrage of lead hot and heavy toward the hated Blackfeet.

Stunned by the attack of reinforcements, the Blackfeet scattered and sought cover.

"Lordy be, Nona! Looks like the calvary has arrived!" Charley exclaimed to his squaw as he picked up another Hawken rifle and poked it through a port to fire.

Nona nodded and kept reloading the rifles.

Charley realized his worst fear when he heard a series of "thunks" hitting the roof of his store. Once he heard a crackling sound, his suspicion was confirmed.

"Nona, git ready to run!" he shouted.

She looked at him with trepidation and fear.

He nodded toward the rafters and shouted angrily, "Set us on fire, they did."

Her mouth dropped open as her eyes cut to the ceiling and panic set in.

He smiled at her and added, "We'll hold out as long as we can. Hopefully, whoever is out there will make themselves known soon."

Taking a deep breath, she nodded.

"Hey! They's setting fire to Charley's!" yelled Packy.

Watching the flames consume their friend's post, Micah elbowed Johan, "You take one side, I'll take the other. Meet around back. Let's get these bastards."

"Ya!"

Glancing across at the others, Micah added, "James, You and Packy see what you can do ta douse that fire."

Two men leaped over the deadfall and ran in a crouch toward each side of the store. They could feel the heat already. Plastered against the wood, each man slithered closer to the back corners of the building.

Johan peered closely into thick growth, looking for his prey. Spotting several, he lunged for cover about ten yards away.

Micah spotted smoke spiraling into the windless air as the Blackfeet ignited their flaming arrows. He dived to his right.

Worn knee-high moccasins stealthily made their way behind three braves. Johan stopped and studied his prey before inching closer to the one in front of him. He made nary a sound. He lunged, wrapped his arm around the brave's neck and covered his mouth with a huge mitt to muffle any sounds of a struggle. Johan drove his Bowie knife deep into the man's side and twisted it, stilling the redskin. Glancing quickly around, he dragged the lifeless body deeper into the underbrush and left it.

↔

James and Packy raced to get the fire contained.

Packy yanked furs from the front of the trading post and tossed them into the water trough.

James jumped the steps, rushed the door yelling and pounded hard, "Charley! Nona! It's me, James! Open up!" he hollered.

Tossing the soaked hides onto the shingled top, Packy shimmied up a post, scrambling onto the blazing roof and began beating the flames with the wet hides.

James heard gagging and coughing behind the door. He banged again and yelled, "Open up!"

Hearing the brace being lifted from the other side, James stepped back and rammed his shoulder into the door, splintering it from its iron hinges and flattened the couple on the inside. Thick smoke roiled before Charley and Nona stumbled out, coughing and retching as they tried to replenish their lungs with fresh air.

Keeping a crouched position, Micah edged closer, silently maneuvering behind the marauders with deadly intent.

The wind was quiet.

All he could smell and hear was the crackling of the blaze consuming Charley's store and home. The sky was becoming infused with smoke and burning ash. He could see Packy on the roof desperately trying to douse the flames with hides.

Ahead of him, he saw four Blackfeet. They had extinguished their small fire and were stomping on its remaining embers. He took a deep breath and let loose a hideous battle cry as he charged the redskins with Bowie knife clenched tightly in his fist.

Surprised at the abrupt attack, the warriors turned and stormed the stout mountain man.

Micah met them head on, ramming his head into the gut of one and throwing him over his shoulder. He balanced on his toes and readied himself for the next brave. His vision was sharp, alerted by the slightest movement.

Immediately, he found himself surrounded. They circled him like a pack of hungry wolves. Micah knew the game because he and his friends had used a similar tactic before. He didn't know what had happened to Johan but knew the Swede could handle himself. So could James and Packy. Wherever they were, it didn't matter. This fight was his alone. Sipping air, he took the plunge and landed a knuckle-numbing blow to the jaw of his first of his adversaries. The brave went sailing, the thick underbrush cushioning his fall, He was out cold from Micah's fist.

Whirling, Cunningham faced the three remaining warriors. Watching and feeling the tension build, he liked the odds better — three against one.

His eyes flickered with contempt for the Blackfeet. He

took a deep breath and let his shoulders relax. His thighs were as tight as a fiddle string waiting for the right moment to deliver a death blow. His hand gripped the hilt of his knife, waiting for them to spiral into action.

One brave took the unspoken challenge. He danced forward with his knife, side-stepped and took a swipe. Then, he pulled back, teasing the mountain man.

Piercing blue eyes didn't miss the message as the three warriors took turns taunting him. Micah was as rough-hewn as the country he traveled. Facing the savages was nothing new. He wasn't intimidated. Instead, he patiently waited for the redskins to make the first move.

The standoff seemed to last an eternity. Then, he saw it. Barely noticeable, the braves' calf muscles tightened as they shifted their weight to the balls of their feet. Micha crouched lower.

Giving a war cry, the Blackfoot launched the attack.

No stranger to backwoods brawls or feuds in the hills and hollows of Kentucky, Cunningham met them head on.

A fist smashed into a nose. Blood splattered. The brave fell back, yowling and holding his face. His pain only got worse as Cunningham buried his blade in the brave's chest.

The remaining two tried to put Micah between them. He leaped and drove his blade into the side of one brave. He twisted the twelve-inch blade and jerked it free. Next, he whirled on the last brave standing.

They eyeballed each other.

Cunningham tossed the knife from one palm to the other, fingers curling comfortably around the hilt and waited.

Leaving a dead warrior in his wake, Johan went looking for Micah. He found him facing off with one remaining warrior. Three others littered the ground. Two were moving but no longer a threat.

Stealthily, Johan crept up behind the lone brave. His partner's expression remained deadpan, not alerting the redskin to Svenson sneak attack.

The renegade's eyes bulged in surprise when an arm circled his neck choking him. The powerful woodsman lifted the brave off the ground and drove the Bowie into his mid-section. As he sliced upward a gurgling sound broke the stillness of the forest as the warrior's body wilted in death.

Pulling the blade out, Svenson let the dead body crumble to the ground. He grinned at Micah and swiped the knife against his well-worn leather britches, the bright red stain contrasted with the dirty, tanned deerskin.

Rustling noises alerted both men to danger. They turned and brandished their weapons in defense. They relaxed when two braves scattered and fled into the forest.

Spinning slowly, Micah sighed and asked, "The others?"

His Swedish lilt had a light tone when he smiled and answered, "Ya, that was fun. They won't see next sun."

Nodding, Micah glanced at the roof of Charley's store. "Let's go find James and Packy and see what we can do to help Charley."

Rounding the corner of the trading post, the men found James, Charley, and Nona by the water trough. Packy was nowhere in sight.

As Cunningham and the Swede approached, a loud crash and guttural yell came from inside the trading post.

Five heads swiveled in response, and four men leaped up the steps. Charging inside, they found Packy lying on the floor moaning.

James and Micah knelt alongside the woodsman, taking note of the soot coving his face, hands and clothing.

"Packy? You hurt?" Micah asked.

Opening his eyes, he glared at them and said, "Dagnabbit! That's a fool thing to ask. Of course, I'm hurt!" He groaned for emphasis.

Micah grinned and grabbed one arm. He motioned to James to grab the other and said, "C'mon ya ol' buzzard. Up ya go."

"Oh, that hurts," Packy stated

"What hurts?"

"Everything."

"Naw, just a little fall; you'll be all right."

His head swiveled, "The hell ya say! I fell through the damn roof!"

James and Micah continued to ease Packy down the steps, stopping by the water trough.

Micah looked at the trough then at James, wiggling his bushy brows in silent communication.

James grinned.

They lifted Packy, kicking and complaining, over the trough.

"Hey? What you two trying to do? You're gonna kill me!" Packy shouted.

"Naw, just a good soaking for your aches and pains."

Water cascaded over the sides when Packy splashed down, arms and legs flailing every which way. He came up spluttering.

"Why you clay-brained, dizzy-eyed, flop-mouthed plumb-plucked son of a canary…"

James' brows rose to his hairline.

Micah laughed and teased, "Packy, we didn't know you knew so many highfalutin' words."

The woodsman's eyes sent daggers through the air.

Svenson stopped laughing long enough to say, "Ya don't seem no worsen fer da wear, Packy boy."

Turning, Cunningham asked, "Nona, you got a bar of lye soap?"

A smile spread across her sun-kissed skin. Dark eyes twinkled as she nodded and ran back inside the store. She returned shortly and handed Micah the soap.

He tossed it to Packy. "No excuse for not taking a bath now," he said and dodged a spray of water coming from the trough.

Chuckling, Trader Charley thumbed over his shoulder, "Mind if'n you boys stay over for a few days and help me set this place right?"

"Ya. Anything fer you Charley?" Johan began, "Anything a-tall."

"Much obliged." Turning and leading the way inside, he called out, "C'mon men, we ain't got all day!"

"When we're done, I expect the best rye ya got, Charley!" Micah called out as laughter filtered through the busted doorway.

CHAPTER 2

Several weeks later, their restoring of the trading post completed, the four were back at the mountain cabin. Micah Cunningham looked up from the hide he was working and squinted at Packy Woods.

"You jabberin' ta hear the sound of your own voice or are ya tryin' to really say something?" he asked.

Surprised, Packy stopped in mid-sentence and said, "Huh?"

James Lavanier and Johan Svenson glanced at each other and grinned. They had blocked out Packy's constant chatter ages ago.

"I mean you've been runnin' a steady stream from that mouth of yourn for a while," Micah said, picking up his clay pipe and reaching for a leather pouch.

"I have?"

"Uh-huh," Micah replied as he opened it, dipped the pipe inside and scooped it full of finely-ground tobacco.

"Well, I was just talking."

His thumb absentmindedly tamped it tighter into the bowl as his brawny frame rose and walked to the fire blazing in the hearth. Glancing back at Packy, Micah added, "Uh-hu. Just' likin' the sound of your own voice is more like it."

Packy frowned at the big Scotch-Irishman, then returned to sewing a set of fur-lined britches for himself.

Picking up a burning stick, Micah angled the flame toward the pipe, sucked deeply and pulled the fire into the bowl. It ignited as fragrant plumes of smoke spiraled around his head and made a quick downturn into the draft of the flue, pulling it up the chimney. Turning and puffing on the pipe, sharp blue eyes squinted against the smoke circling his face and studied his comrades.

James Lavanier liked to tell people he was of mixed heritage because his people hailed from the West Indies and French Canada. James explained he was the second generation of this mixed blood. Some of his mother's people had come to Canada years ago from the West Indies with French trappers. Like so many others, they sought a new life in an untamed wilderness. She married a French trapper and bore James along with several more children.

James's dark skin didn't look like he had any Canadian in him at all. His coal black eyes and fuzzy hair said it all. Inwardly shrugging to himself, it didn't matter anyway, James' blood was just as red as any. He was a good man and a mighty fine trapper.

Walking to the open doorway of their cabin, Micah stared at the dappled, sun-drenched scene. A small meadow was to his right. A stream below meandered through the forest that surrounded the staked claim. It had a spring that bubbled out of the hill behind the cabin. Puffing on his pipe, he glanced over at their elevated cache. It was built six feet off the ground to hold the furs they would eventually transport. Seasoned meat and other sundries they needed to exist in the untamed wilderness. The little spot the men called home was nestled deep in the southern Rockies and on the western slopes. Years ago, a small trading post had been set up by Trader Charley for the trappers and local tribes to do business. It became known as Sinking Springs for whatever reason. It stuck. A good five days out from there one would find the small homestead.

He glanced over his shoulder at Johan Svenson. The strapping, blond-haired Swede was a giant. He towered over Micah but was as a good partner a man could hope to have. Removing the pipe from his mouth, he tapped the bowl on the side of the cabin, to empty it. After refilling and relighting the pipe, his thoughts meandered to where he and Johan first met.

It was up in Yellowstone country. The hulking Swede was fending off a dozen Assiniboine warriors. He grinned at the memory. Most tribes got along with mountain men, but there were some who didn't like the intrusion. Assiniboine was one of them.

Micah jumped into the fray, sealing a friendship that

had lasted for at least a decade. Micah had lost track but hoped it would continue.

Walking to check on the stock hobbled in the meadow, Packy Woods came to mind. That beanpole was the odd duck in the outfit. Scatterbrained and capable of talking a blue streak, the loner had walked up on the trio's campfire one night. He took a seat next to them and never left.

Tucking the pipe into his britches, he unhobbled the stock and led them to the stream to drink. Kneeling upstream from them, Micah dipped his hand into the clear water and refreshed his thirst. The cold mountain water invigorated his innards.

As he waited for the horses to finish, he let blue eyes scan the homestead. It wasn't much but in a couple of years it would be Johan's and his if they kept proving it up.

Having had their fill of water, the animals moseyed off to graze. The sound of grass being ripped and chewed satisfied his soul. After leaving Kentucky and landing in the Rockies, Micah knew he had found where he belonged. He would live and die here.

He strode back to the cabin and his comrades. A steaming cup of coffee was calling him.

The last of the heavy winter snowpack had given up with the warming days. Only trace amounts remained in the deep forest shade.

The sun felt good on the winter chilled bones of the four mountain men as they went about individual chores.

James would be heading out to Powder River Basin in a few days. Packy planned on taking the last of the stored hides down to Trader Charley's and give him a list of supplies they would need for the coming months. A freighter captain, Mushy Drummond, would be arriving soon on his first of two yearly trips to Sinking Springs.

Johan had packed his clay pipe and was enjoying the scent of tobacco wafting past his nose. He sat in a chair and leaned back against the side of the cabin, basking in the warn sunshine.

"Charley said that Mushy Drummond told him folks is a hankering for more buff hides back East," he said to his partners."

Cunningham pulled the stem of his pipe from his lips, cut a glance at the strapping Swede and replied, "You don't say?"

"Ya."

"No more beaver or wolf hides?"

"Ya, still those. But buff hides are favored," Johan said.

"I wouldn't mind some buffalo hump to eat on this winter," Packy added.

"That's Crow and Lakota country," Micah remarked. "They might not take too kindly to folks skinning out their food supply."

"Cheyenne, too," James added.

Svenson shrugged, tapping his pipe against his leg, emptying the bowl and refilling it.

"Tis true, but tanners are paying double for the buff hides, according to Mushy," the big Swede said. He struck a match against wood and sucked the flame deep into the fresh tobacco.

"It'd be good money," he added, letting the word money hang in the air.

His eyes drifted to the peaceful scene in front of the cabin, the sunlight sparkling like diamonds on the river below. Their stock was happily munching on the high, lush grass.

"Y'all is welcome ta come with me, if'n you be hankering fer some buff hides to parley with," James said.

Three pairs of eyes gazed at Lavanier, then at each other.

"You three go ahead," Packy began. "I'll take what we got left down to Charley's and catch up with ya at some point."

CHAPTER  3

"There she be boys, the Powder River Basin," Lavanier nodded toward the sprawling vista.

The land stretched for miles, imitating a wrinkled quilt with its rolling hills, short peaks and shallow valleys. The native grasses were bending to the will of the wind. Trees, outfit in their full summer dressage, were scattered everywhere the eye roamed. Ancient granite escarpments dotted the landscape, seeming to pop out of the ground at will. The sky was a deep blue, pockmarked with a few billowing clouds that forecasted good weather for the next few days.

Micah leaned forward, resting a forearm on the saddle horn. He enjoyed the soft caress of the wind against his face. It ruffled his long dark whiskers like feathers on a bird. Straightening, he breathed deeply. The air was fresh and filled with more scents than he could count. All were pleasing to his nose.

There was nothing quite like the smell of green grass in its summer glory. Of course, it contrasted with the smell of well-used leather and the musky scent of their mounts and pack mules. Pockets of wildflowers danced gaily in the soft wind. Nonetheless, Micah sighed inwardly loving every second of it.

Johan had been skirting the scene with his blue eyes. The dark dots of the buffalo herd stretched for miles, accented by the lighter colored coats of the antelope that tagged along. What he was looking for he didn't find. No Indians were following behind the herd, waiting to strike. He also didn't smell the chip smoke that would signal their presence. Buffalo droppings could be used to make a quick fire in a pinch.

Johan's Swedish lilt broke the silence. "Appears the tribes haven't made it to their summer hunting grounds," he said, glancing at Micah and James. "Good timing."

A smile broke across ebony skin, "Yup," replied James.

Puckering his lips, Micah nodded in agreement. "Let's find a good spot for a base camp and set up. Tomorrow will be a busy day," he said.

Nudging their mounts, the men angled down the ridge through belly high grasses as they searched for a suitable camp.

Two hours later the three mountain men reined up and surveyed an appealing spot. There was a dusty wallowing hole for the buffalo on the other side of a four-foot stream.

A sizeable rock edifice, located about fifteen feet from the water, lent some protection from the elements.

"Maybe we could just sit in our bedrolls and drop them when they come to visit." James said.

"Ya, I like this place," Johan agreed.

Micah looked pointedly at Lavanier and asked, "You hunted here before?"

James just grinned.

"A few," he said as he slipped out of the leather and led his mount to the stream.

A base camp was quickly established. Each of the seasoned hunters knew their duties without speaking a word.

Looking around and spitting a stream of brown juice at an unseen target, James remarked, "Least we don't have ta go looking for fuel. Them buffs was kind enough to drop them patties right in our yard."

"Right neighborly," Johan added.

"Well, get moving then." Micah threw out. "I'm hankering for some hot coffee."

Darkness slithered in silently, clothing the camp like a shroud. The buffalo chip fire barely highlighted the men's rugged faces. The sky glittered with millions of diamonds.

The wind had died, leaving just the occasional soft caress against their features. With the heat of the day gone, the air carried a chill to it.

Johan and James were already snoring softly. Micah smiled faintly at the sound. His thoughts drifted to Packy, and he wondered how he was getting along.

He should be on his way.

It had taken them ten days to traverse the distance, but the rewards would be great. Tapping the dead embers from his pipe, Micah settled down for sleep. Tomorrow promised to be a good day.

With their short barrel .50/80 caliber Hawken rifles at their sides, the trio stepped out of their saddles and began walking closer to the herd. The grass swished against their leather britches releasing the heavy dew and leaving damp spots.

A slim line of color crawled across the horizon to the east, illuminating the hundreds of buffalo fifty yards ahead. The herd was slowly munching their way west in the basin. Two bulls faced off in a ramming contest, sending dust billowing and clumps of turf flying. Theirs was a quest for supremacy.

Mourning doves, hawks and quail broke the stillness with their cacophony of chatter.

Twenty-five yards from the herd, the men stopped and dropped to their bellies. Arms reached out to split the grasses forming an unprecedented view of their prey.

Obsidian colored eyes, along with two sets of blue, scanned the slight rise on the other side of the buffalo. It appeared they were the only hunters in the area. It was customary for tribes to follow the great herds, but they had not arrived yet for their summer hunts.

Preparing their rifles, the men picked their targets and took aim. Suddenly, they were distracted by the sound of pounding hooves heading in their direction. They lowered their rifles and gazed eastward.

"What the hell?" whispered Lavanier.

Cunningham's eyes narrowed when he saw a lone rider reach the ridge and tear down the hill. "Damn fool! What the hell is he doing?"

"That rider is gonna make them buffs spook and run," added Johan.

James nodded, "Look how lathered that horse is. He's been running for a while."

"He's mad," injected Svenson. "Can't ride that close to them buffs."

"Something sure has him all in a tither," Micah remarked. He rose suddenly and added, "Gonna see what's going on."

He ran back to his horse, jumped into the saddle and

kicked the mount into a run. He rode past James and Johan like a whirlwind.

The bay and its rider cut a path between the hunters and the herd. Micah rode low over his mount's neck and urged the red roan into a faster pace. He inched closer to the lone rider.

Unexpectantly, the horse squealed in pain, tumbled and flipped in the air. It landed on its back, pinning the rider underneath.

Micah looked quickly toward the herd and noted a few horned heads jerk up in response to the horse's cry of distress, but thousands of hooves hadn't hit the ground in a startled stampede just yet.

Cunningham reached the downed rider and jumped clear of his mount. He slid his hands under the man's armpits and pulled him from beneath the 1,200 pounds of thrashing horse flesh.

The rider was unconscious and appeared unharmed. The thick turf must have cushioned his fall

The bay's leg was broken from stepping into a gopher hole. There was nothing Micah could do for the animal. The only thing left was something he did not want to do, but he would not let the horse suffer any longer. Whipping out his knife, he slit the creature's throat. Blood spurted. The animal squealed again, tried to right itself and slowly lost energy as its blood drained, staining the green grass bright red.

James and Johan rode hard to assist Micah.

Looking at the unconscious rider, Micah realized it wasn't a man but a boy. The lanky lad had reddish-brown hair. Ruddy skin accented the freckles on his forehead, cheeks and nose. His clothing was well worn. A faded muslin shirt was tucked into corded britches that were thread-bare and glossy-looking. Suspenders hung over thin shoulders. He wore what Micah called city shoes, the soles worn thin and the tops scuffed.

Hearing hoofbeats he glanced up just as the others arrived.

"It's a kid," Micah announced.

"Nice piece of horseflesh," James noted. "Too bad you had to do that."

Micah looked at him and explained, "Had no choice." Nodding at the dead horse, he added, "Get that saddle and bridle off. We'll take the kid back to camp."

Micah's head swung, studying the herd, "Need to put some distance between us and them, should they decide to move," he stated.

"Ya, good idea," Johan grinned.

As they waited for the boy to wake up, the three slurped stale coffee and smoked. Lavanier broke off a fresh chew softening it with his saliva and enjoyed the smoky flavor.

A groan got their attention, and three heads swung toward the youngster. Stirring slowly, the boy gradually sat up. As his eyes gained focus, he spotted his rescuers and broke into a cheek-splitting grin.

"Thank God! I thought I'd never find anyone," the boy declared. When he spotted a canteen, he asked, "Can I have some water?"

Removing the pipe from his lips, Micah handed over the canteen and said, "Lot of lonesome ground out here."

Brown eyes darted around the small camp, "Where's my horse."

"Stepped in a gopher hole. We had to dispose of it," Micah said.

"What were you doing riding hell-bent for Purgatory, anyways?" asked James.

The boy's eyes swung in the direction of the dark-skinned mountain man, and he asked, "You their slave?"

Chuckles greeted his comment.

The kid frowned.

"Free man, boy. Same as you."

"You got a name?" Micah inquired.

The lad nodded and said, "JP."

"JP what?"

"Thigpen."

"Where ya from?"

"Wagon train, 'bout half-days ride that-a-way," he pointed to the ridge behind the herd. "We came under attack, the wagon master sent me for help. We's on our way to the Oregon Territory."

"What's this wagon master's name?" Micah asked.

"Decker Curtright."

"That piece of back-water, side-winding hide ain't fit ta lead a train of greenhorns!" Johan snorted.

"Can you ride, boy?"

"I think so."

"Saddle up then. Let's see what kinda mess Curtright put your poor folks in, JP."

CHAPTER 4

Topping a short ridge, the riders surveyed the scene below. The wagon train was still strung out. Dead Indians were scattered across the plains. The bodies of some of the defenders could be seen alongside wagons. Some stock had perished, and five wagons were a total loss.

"We had more stock but the Indians ran off with a slew of 'em," JP informed.

"Damned Curtright!" Johan muttered softly. "The fool didn't even circle the wagons."

Pointing toward the far rise, James nodded and said, "There they are. We best get down there and help those folks get ready."

Their eyes slid from the disaster below to the band of renegades watching and waiting.

An unspoken signal seemed to pass between them as their heels gouged the ribs of their mounts and they took off toward the train. Their pack mules kept pace but JP had to keep digging heels into his mules' sides to encourage it to keep up.

Nearing the train, the youngster surged ahead yelling, "Don't shoot! Don't shoot! I got help!"

Folks came out of hiding. Women and children poked their heads through tattered canvas, a mix of fear and relief etched across weary faces. The men pointed their muzzles downward as they watched the four gallop toward them. Dust covered many of the settlers' faces.

A thick Swedish accent broke the quiet as Svenson bellowed, "Who's the damn ramrod in charge?"

A thick-set man stepped out from behind a wagon with a spread stance with a rifle resting in the crook of his arm. He was dressed in buckskins, much like the men who sat astride their horses and glared at him in disgust.

He wore a short-crowned, floppy hat with a band made from the skin of a rattlesnake. Stained with sweat and dirt, it sat atop long stringy hair. He had dark, beady eyes and a crooked nose. A long beard, streaked with tobacco dribbles, covered most of his to pock-marked cheeks.

"I am!" he called out angrily and spat a string of brown juice for emphasis.

Svenson who had a long-standing history with the side-winding wagon master, leaned forward over the neck of his bay and spit forth challenging words,

"Taking advantage of these greenhorns, are ya, Curtright?" he shouted. "Killing 'em off. so's ya can rob 'em?"

Micah interceded before hostilities could break out.

"We ain't got much time. You folks pull them wagons into a circle and unhitch your stock," he ordered. Then he glanced at Curtright and added, "You were a damn fool for leaving these wagons like this."

He didn't wait for a response. He turned the roan and began barking more orders at the naïve settlers.

Svenson followed, but issued a warning over his shoulder, "Your day is coming, Curtright!"

JP ran to help his father turn his family's wagon. He climbed into the box seat and said, "Pa, I did it. Found us some help."

His father's hand reached out, tousled the boy's hair as he said, "That you did, son. I'm proud and grateful."

Looking over his shoulder at the inside of the wagon and the partially torn canvas, JP observed, "Guess we fared better than some others."

Nodding, his father added, "We did. We are blessed. I've asked Mrs. Livingston to share the wagon."

"Did they lose everything?"

"Almost, including her husband," the elder Thigpen said.

JP grimaced.

The boy hopped down from the seat of the prairie schooner after his father had fallen into line with the other settlers' wagons. He unhitched the stock and let them loose in the confines of the circle.

James walked over to where Johan and Micah were standing, forearms resting comfortably across the muzzles of their Hawken rifles. They closely supervised the bustling activity, while keeping an eye on the warriors who were poised to attack from the ridge.

"Think we need to take stock of what supplies these folks got? We might be in for a long haul before we can move on again." James said.

Johan swung his gaze to the ridge, "Hunting party or war party?" he asked of no one in particular.

Obsidian eyes turned into slits to focus on the distant rise. "Might be both," James replied.

"I think they know that buff herd is ahead. Let's hope they are more interested in gathering food supplies than this wagon train," added Micah.

Svenson looked at the sky. Red, yellow, and purple hues were beginning to crawl across the western horizon. Stars were beginning to show to the east.

"Them redskins won't attack at night. Against their religion," he grinned. "Gives us time to see what we got for food and water, give these folks a rest and get ready for them in the morning."

He nodded toward Curtright and added with a devilish grin, "Sides, it'll give me time to knock some sense into that sidewinder's head."

Micah gave the big Swede a squirrely look and warned, "Don't go biting off more'n you can chew."

"Ha!" the Swede retorted. "Why, I can lick him with my little finger." He stuck the small digit in the air for emphasis.

James chuckled, shaking his head in amusement. He knew Johan spoke the truth. The two walked off to check the supplies of the settlers.

CHAPTER 5

It had been a long haul, and Packy Woods was tired when he reined up his dingy white mule. He was the only one of the four mountain men who preferred riding a mule instead of a horse, claiming they were more suited for the mountainous terrain. They were not much for speed, but excellent for a long haul. The three pack mules behind him snorted, grateful for the breather.

He had been riding fifty yards out and alongside one of the largest buffalo herds he had ever seen. His alert eyes scanned the area, looking for his friends and keeping a watchful eye for native hunting parties. So far, he hadn't sighted either.

Something flickered in his peripheral vision. He turned slightly to the right and spotted a flock of vultures that had discovered something to feast upon. Wings beat the air as the scavengers jostled for tidbits. He reined the mule in that direction.

As he approached, the buzzards scattered, their voices protesting his intrusion on their meal. Packy, lean and rangy, was surprised when he came upon the decomposing and mutilated body of a horse. He had no idea how long the horse had been dead; the prairie foragers had pretty much picked the carcass clean.

Frowning, he looked at the turf for sign. His eyes picked out faint tracks leading away from the area. So, he nudged the mule with his heels and followed them.

When he spotted the dirt wallow and the small stream, Packy dismounted and let the mules drink their fill before proceeding across to a granite outcrop. He studied the vacant campsite, wondering if it was his comrades who had stopped there. He squatted before the day-old fire ring and sifted through the warm ashes. Buff chips kept heat longer than wood. Deciding it would be a good place to rest, he unpacked the panniers and hobbled his mules. He hankered for a good sleep.

Ready to roll as the sun crested the eastern horizon, Woods stepped into the leather and settled comfortably into the well-worn seat. He nudged the mule forward and continued his quest to find Johan, Micah and James.

The buffalo herd had moved farther west during the night, the mass fanning out for more of the lush grasses.

Scanning the countryside, he still saw no sign of summer hunting parties. He frowned, trying to remember what month it was. The last he could recollect it was the middle or end of May when he was at Trader Charley's. So, it should be June? He took off his cap and scratched his head and pondered in it.

Darned, if I remember.

His eyes appreciatively took in the size of the herd as he rode east, picking up the trail as it left the camp. His mouth watered thinking about all that good meat just sitting on four hooves. He sighed, knowing his hunger would have to wait until he caught up with his comrades.

As the train settled in, Micah checked in at the Thigpen wagon to make sure all was well. JP's father stepped forward and said, "Thanks for saving my son. I'm Willis Thigpen." He offered his hand and added, "Won't you take supper with us?"

Micah studied the man, nodded and said, "That would be kindly."

Willis Thigpen had his son's ruddy and freckled skin, a square face and reddish-brown hair. His clothes were as worn as his son's. He wore boots with shabby pants legs shoved haphazardly into the tops of the scuffed leather.

Turning, Thigpen addressed his son, "JP, get out some cups and plates for these men."

"Yes, sir!" the lad replied.

The three sat cross-legged around the chip fire, each savoring a cup of welcoming coffee. They slurped and relaxed.

The silence stretched while they ate a meal of beans and biscuits.

Setting his plate down and refilling his cup, Thigpen opened the conversation. "Where you men from?"

"Sinking Springs," Micah said.

"Where's that?"

"Southern range of the Rocky Mountains."

"You came a far piece then."

Nodding, Micah said, "We was hunting buffalo."

Thigpen's mind chewed on that for a bit before asking, "How long do you think we'll be stuck here?"

Cunningham and Lavanier shrugged.

Johan replied, "Depends."

"On what?" Thigpen asked.

"Don't know."

"Well, that's a hell of answer," their host muttered in dismay.

JP's eyes bounced from his father to the three mountain men and back again.

Digging his clay pipe out and filling it with tobacco, Micah said, "You got enough water, shot and powder to last two days if them redskins keep you pinned down." Micah

45

struck the match against his leather britches and held the flame over the bowl while he looked Thigpen in the eye. "After that? Your trek most likely ends here, your dead body melting into the land, like many before you."

He opened his mouth to say more, but James interceded. "There's a big buffalo herd a little more'n half-a-day's ride west of here," he informed.

JP nodded and added, "That's right, Pa. I seen 'em. There were hundreds of them. I never saw the end of the herd in any directions."

"Ya, tis many," Johan agreed.

Lavanier spoke up, hoping to explain. "We figure them Indians don't want you finding that herd. That's why they attacked," he said.

Frowning, Thigpen asked, "Ain't there enough for everyone?"

"Not the way they see it," Micah returned as he puffed away.

"The tribes can be mighty territorial when it comes to food," Johan snorted, filling his pipe again with tobacco. "Where in the hell did you pick up that rascal you call a wagon master?"

"Um... we found him in St Joe. Me and my boy traveled from Ohio to there," he said.

"How much did that sidewinder take y'all fer?"

Thigpen took offense and bristled, "That ain't none of yer business!"

Dipping his head, Svenson chuckled. Cutting a slanted glance at the settler, he stated flatly, "That much, huh?"

James broke in before it escalated. "Excuse our friend. Him and Curtright go back a way, and they ain't particularly friends."

Throwing a dirty look at the Swede, Micah added his two-cents worth. "Think it's time for you two to get some sleep."

"What about you three?' asked JP.

"We sleep standing up," he teased, rising to his full height of six feet plus. Looking at the boy's father, he added, "Thanks for the meal."

Thigpen nodded, beginning to roll out their blankets.

JP's eyes popped. "You do?"

Lavanier snickered and explained, "He means we're doing night patrol."

"Oh."

Reaching for the rifle leaning against the wheel of the schooner, Johan grinned and said, "Ya, keeps us on our toes that way."

JP smiled back.

The men stepped over the wagon tongue, rifles cradled in their arms, and began to leisurely circle the wagons.

After their third round, Johan, Micah and James met up to discuss the travelers' dilemma.

"They ain't gonna be able to take another raid. There's women and children here."

Johan looked at the sky. "If I recollect right, it's somewheres between ten or eleven."

Micah glanced up also gauging the time and said, "You thinkin' we ought to roust 'em and move out under the cover of darkness?"

"Yup."

"Them cayuses won't move until daylight." James added. "We could put some distance betwixt them and us."

"Curtright ain't gonna like it."

A grin busted through Micah's thick beard. "Just slug him. Gag him, tie him up and throw him in the back of his freight wagon," Micah said. "Think you could take care of that?"

A broad smile plastered Johan's face, "Ya, it'll be fun."

Warning the travelers to keep quiet and work as quickly as possible to break camp in the dark, the three men got their own mounts and pack mules ready.

Checking the situation one more time, Johan rounded the corner of a freight wagon, running smack-dab into

Decker Curtright.

Curtright snarled, "What the hell do you think you're doing?"

"Movin' out," Svenson replied.

"Like hell! This is my wagon train!" he barked.

Quick as a lightning bolt, Johan's fist met the man's face. Cartilage cracked. Blood spurted as the wagon master yowled and landed hard on his backside. Eyes blinking and watering, he cradled his nose, trying to ease the intense pain.

"It was 'til we showed up," Johan declared with a simple reply. Looking at the Curtright's helper, who cowered under the wagon, Johan ordered, "Get your man to hitch your team. We're moving out in fifteen minutes."

He spun and walked off with a faint smile gracing his blonde stubble.

Shaking off help from his driver, Curtright stumbled over to the water bucket and poured all of it on his throbbing face. Staring at the Swede's broad back walking away, the wagon master swore quietly, "Damn you, Svenson. You'll be a dead man first chance I get."

CHAPTER  6

No moon lighted their way; only a million sparkling diamond-like stars penetrated the darkness as the settlers crawled along. No one spoke. It was as if their breath might awaken the enemy and hasten their doom. Trace chains jingled slightly. Wheel hubs creaked with each turn. Teams of four and two pulled the schooners and wagons, plodding through damp grasses and heading deeper into the western territories.

James rode alongside the lead wagon. Johan on the right mid-way down and Micah rode drag. His companion was Curtright. His freight wagon brought up the rear. He kept stealing glances at the man's swollen-pulpy face and hiding a gratifying grin. Johan had been true to his word.

Only ten wagons remained from the original fifteen. Settlers had doubled up offering refuge and accommodation to those who were burned out.

The train was small in comparison to some of the wagon processions that frequently bisected The Great Plains. They were filled with newcomers, who sought the promise of free land and spearheaded the nation's westward expansion.

The hairs on the back of his neck no longer flared, but that didn't keep Cunningham from throwing a watchful eye to the ridges behind. Once the renegades figured out they were gone, they would come swooping down on them in a hurry. Looking at the sky, he figured they had a few more hours before daylight.

A half-hour before dawn, Johan called a halt. Stock was watered, as well as travelers. Then, they were on the move again.

James rode back to check in with Micah. Not seeing Curtright, he asked, "Where's that scalawag?"

"Up there," Micah said and pointed. Curtright had moved up in the procession.

Finding him out of earshot, James voiced his concern: "There's nothing but prairie for hundreds of miles. No trees to protect us from the next attack."

"I know," Micah answered.

"Aren't you curious why Curtright took this route instead of one most others do? Ain't no protection or chance to re-stock 'til Fort Hall. That's a good twenty days out or more as slow as wagons move."

"Been thinking along those lines, too," Micah agreed, looking at the tailgate of the freight wagon before him.

"Been wondering what he's hauling. That might be the reason for the attack and not the buff herd up yonder."

Pursing his lips, James pondered the possibilities and finally said, "That's possible."

"Those renegades attacked for a reason. Why? Most Injuns get curious when folks cross their land. They watch but pretty much leave 'em alone unless provoked."

He shook his head and then added, looking James straight in the eye. "What they did back there wasn't normal."

Lavanier nodded and replied, "Makes ya wonder if Curtright left his passengers open to attack on purpose."

His friend paused again to gather his thoughts; then he said, "Or Curtright has somethin' for the Indians and has not held up his end of the bargain."

"Hmmm?"

On impulse, Micah rode closer to the back of the wagon. Tossing the reins to James, he nimbly grabbed the edge and pulled himself onto the tarp covering the contents.

Hearing a noise behind him, the driver glanced over his shoulder and gave the mountain man an angry look.

"Hey! What do you think you're doing?" he challenged.

Ignoring the voice, Micah kept cutting the rope holding down the canvas.

Dropping the reins, the driver scrambled back and attacked the woodsman, who knocked him flat.

The four-up wasn't sure what was happening and picked up their pace. The team of horses went from a plodding walk to a trot and a full gallop. Fear fed their momentum.

Quickly, James released the reins of Micah's horse and rode several lengths to the box seat. Kicking feet free of the stirrups, his hands latched onto the runaway freight seat. Muscles bulged as he tried to keep his legs from being tangled in the furiously spinning wheel. He managed to gain leverage and haul himself into the seat.

The wagon careened out of control, bypassing the rest of the train and turning away.

Mouths dropped open as settlers reined in their own teams and watched the runaway wagon.

Whirling his mount, Curtright charged after the freight wagon, too.

Johan urged his bay into a turf eating run.

The driver was no match for Cunningham. Micah picked him up and tossed him from the top of the racing freight. He bounced when he hit the ground and laid still.

Micah wasted no time in crawling over the cargo to James. "Where's the reins?"

James pointed. They were dragging on the ground.

Micah looked. It was too dangerous to climb down and retrieve them behind flying hooves. He glanced up. The racing teams were headed for a barely visible granite outcropping. He knew immediately what was about to happen.

James was gauging the distance to leap onto the back of one of the horses when Micah's hand clutched his shoulder to draw his attention. He didn't mince any words. "Jump!" he yelled.

They both almost waited too long before clearing the seat. Their feet hit the ground first. Then, they dropped and rolled with the momentum. They popped back up just in time to see the cargo shift, causing the wagon to tilt to one side. Still hitched, the teams rose in the air as the heavy weight flipped the wagon over. The intensity of its speed kept it skidding, raking dirt and turf along until it finally slid to a stop. The horses struggled against the restraining harnesses, screaming in agony. Wheels spun furiously as the contents of the wagon scattered. Barrels hit the rocks and split open. Others rolled. Bags of flour and sugar split open and dusted the prairie grass.

Johan raced to rescue the distressed team, as did James and Micah. Together, they untangled each horse and led them away. One they were unable to save. A knife to the throat drained its life onto the ground.

Enraged, Curtright leaped from his horse and advanced upon Cunningham. A palm landed heavy on

Micah's shoulder and jerked the woodsman around to face the besieged wagon master.

Fighting instincts kicked in. The driving force from Curtright helped Micah to land a punishing blow to the man's jaw, cracking his knuckles in the process. The head of the train leader snapped to the left, a wad of tobacco flying from his mouth as he stumbled and reeled backward. He landed hard on his shoulder.

Crouching and balanced on the balls of his feet, Micah waited for the next onslaught.

The wagon train had long since stopped, and settlers had abandoned their wagons. Drawn to the entertainment, they formed a semi-circle around the fighting men.

Knowing Micah could take care of himself, James wandered over to the busted cargo and began sifting through it. He upturned some of the barrels and stacked kegs, some of which had rolled ten feet but were unharmed. Suddenly, the early morning sunlight reflected off something and grabbed his attention. Shoving busted wooden debris away, James gave a low whistle at what he saw. Glancing over his shoulder, he called out, "Johan! Micah! Come see what I found!"

Svenson began walking toward James.

Micah's head swiveled when he heard his name called. Curtright took the opportunity to slam full bore into his enemy's side. They both tangled in the dirt.

The woodsman grunted from the blow but scrambled to regain his footing and leverage. The two pummeled each other. The fight turned into a donnybrook that attracted the settlers.

Micah shielded his face as much as possible, but the action was furious. When something sharp pierced his upper arm, he knew he'd been sliced. He smelled the copper scent of his own blood as it trickled down his arm and soaked his buckskin shirt. Rage helped him block the pain.

Curtright backed off. Hate filled the man's eyes, fueled by old history. A snarl graced his lips as he waited for Cunningham to make the next move.

Taking a deep breath, Micah decided to disarm his opponent verbally before striking again.

"Ach! Ya be a sly one, Curtright," he said, laying on the thick brogue. He nodded toward the knife in his hand and added, "And yer a bit wicked with ya Bowie, I admit."

Straightening his short stature, the wagon master tossed the hilt of the Bowie from one palm to the other.

"That I am," he said threateningly. He thought he heard fear in the mountain man's voice. It fueled his confidence.

Micah judged the distance between them. He had an old trick up his sleeve; but needed to be a tad closer. As he paced forward, he distracted Curtright with his words,

"I do believe you might have beaten me this time," he

jested.

Apprehension filled his opponent's eyes. He licked his dry lips and said, "Not until you and Svenson is both dead will I rest. And kill you, I will."

Throwing his chest out and arms wide, Micah taunted, "Well, here I am."

Hesitating for a fraction of a second, Curtright made his move.

His thigh muscles tightened as Cunningham leaped into the air, both moccasin-clad feet slammed into his opponents' chest, Curtright was knocked backward five feet and landed hard. Breath gushed from his mouth in a loud whoosh, as his Bowie went flying from his hand.

Pouncing on Curtright, Micah flipped him over on his belly and pulled a forearm up high behind his back.

Grunting and trying to suck air, Curtright struggled to get free.

Pulling his own knife, Cunningham laid it against the wagon master's throat.

Curtright immediately stilled.

Straddling and rising, Micah jerked on the arm, shoving it farther behind his back.

The joint was about to pop when Curtright surrendered. "All right! All right!" he bellowed.

"Up!" Micah ordered.

CHAPTER 7

With all eyes focused on the slugfest, nobody noticed the visitors approaching. It was JP who spotted them out of the corner of his eye. He grabbed his father's shirtsleeve and whispered, "Pa! Look! They're back!" He pointed in the direction they had just traveled.

Several women heard his words, looked and screamed. Immediately, they ran for the wagons with children in tow.

James and Johan whirled, wondering why the women were screeching. Visitors were arriving at the most inopportune time.

The Adam's apple in Willis Thigpen's throat bobbed up and down when he saw who was riding up. Whirling, he ran to Johan and James, flailing his arm in the air and shouting, "They're back! They're back!"

The woodsmen instantly noticed the non-threatening slow approach.

"Ya, we see 'em," responded Johan.

"Don't run for your guns," James warned. "And get

those women and children back. They are safer here, than hiding in them wagons."

Turning, James and Johan made their way back to the flipped freight hauler and the circle of settlers. Micah noticed the visitors and zeroed in on the overexcited Thigpen. He shoved the wagon master toward him and ordered him to bind him. "Do it good and tight, too!" he added.

Walking closer to Johan and James, he spoke softly, "Where did they come from?"

Folding his arms over a burley chest, Johan's blond brow spiked and he said, "Too busy fighting for yer honor ta notice?"

Micah threw the woodsman a hard look.

Johan grinned.

James nodded toward the spilled freight revealed, "Curtright was hauling Hawken rifles."

Micah looked at his partner with shocked eyes.

"You don't say?" he said. Then, he walked over and picked up one of the rifles from a broken box and gave a low whistle.

"Powder and shot too, among other things."

Cradling the rifle in his arms, he walked back toward his friends and asked, "James, you think them Crow?"

A band of twenty Indians sat atop ponies about thirty

feet away and silently watched the travelers.

"Yeah," James replied.

"Looks ta me they be wanting to parley," Johan added.

"And I'll just bet I know who they come to meet with, too."

Johan looked at Curtright trussed up like a hog, "Ya, me too."

James nodded. "More'n likely he intended to deliver them rifles this trip; but decided to keep 'em for himself. Hoping for a higher pay day at Fort Hall."

"Maybe?"

A sodbuster stepped forward and asked, "When you men gonna do something 'bout them damn Indians?"

The three turned at once and stared at the settler.

"Nothin'," said Micah. "They's just sitting peaceable like. No sense riling them up and gettin' us all killed."

"Well, if you ain't gonna do something, I am," he said, spinning on the balls of his feet and heading for his wagon. Before he got too far away, Micah lunged and slammed the butt of the Hawken into the back of the man's head. He dropped like a rock, out cold.

A short cry lifted through the air as a woman flew out of the crowd and knelt by her husband. Sending an evil stare to the three woodsmen. Her eyes filled with hatred when they fell on Micah.

"You dirty, filthy, despicable piece of human waste," she screamed.

"Yessum, I might be that. But us three is all ya got between you and them," he said, thumbing over his shoulder, "Death can be a bit painful at the hands of one on them Injuns."

Blue eyes pierced the rest of the crowd and Micah called out, "The rest of you stay put. We'll handle this."

Packy Woods was surprised when he topped the rise. He jerked his dingy white mule to a stop. Surveying the scene below, he wasn't sure he liked what he saw. A crowd of people standing around a flipped schooner, twenty Indians thirty yards to the north and a wagon train up ahead. His grimy face pulled into a frown. He had never seen the likes of it. Studying the bystanders, he could just make out his friends. Nudging the mule and pulling the packtrain, he made a beeline for them, hoping the Indians wouldn't attack.

Seeing a horse and rider flying toward them, JP called out, "Mister Cunningham, look!"

The woodsmen turned.

"Why, I'll be. It's Packy!" he shouted with surprise.

Sliding to a stop, Packy sucked in wind, "What you boys got yourself into this time? I swear, I gotta keep digging ya out of scrapes."

He thumbed over his shoulder, he added, "And what's them cayuses doing sitting pretty as ya please?"

Micha grinned and said, "Still rawboned and ugly as ever…"

"Ya, still talkin' a blue streak, too," James added.

"Yins just lucky I showed up a-tall," retorted Packy.

"Light down," James gestured. "You're just in time."

Slipping out of the leather, Packy asked, "In time fer what?"

Motioning for JP to come forward, Micah said, "Son, take Packy's mules over yonder, would you kindly?"

Nodding, the lad did as he was told.

Squinting and pushing his hat back on his head, Packy let his eyes roam over the situation. Bumfuzzled, Woods turned to his comrades and asked, "How the hell did you hook up with a wagon train? Thought you was buff hunting?"

"Uh, we was… er will be." James offered. "Soon as this mess is straightened out."

"And a powerful mess it seems to be, I reckon," Packy observed.

"Reckon these good folks' wagon master plumb forgot to keep his word to them braves over yonder," Micah explained. "Err… that's what we think."

Packy took his hat off, scratched his head in puzzlement and said, "Huh?"

James explained further, "Decker Curtright apparently promised them Crows these Hawken rifles."

Packy snorted and snarled, "Why that Decker Curtright ain't got an honest bone in his lying body!"

He did a doubletake and asked, "Did you say Hawken rifles?"

"Ya."

"Damn, figure Curtright'd be up to no good. I'd like me a new Hawken, but not from the likes of him," Packy said.

Another settler stepped forward to interrupt their conversation. His voice was edgy as he insisted, "Are you men gonna do something 'bout them damn Injuns 'fore they kill us? Or you gonna stand there flapping your jaws all day?"

"James? You know any Crow?" Micah asked.

"Not per-say but sign ought to work."

"Let's go 'fore these greenhorns provoke a war."

The four hunters walked toward the party of Crow. Micah raised the rifle overhead and parallel with the ground in a none-threatening pose as they approached the Crow party.

The braves waited silently. Only their horses showed impatience.

Stopping ten paces from them, the woodsmen and Crow eyeballed each other. The braves wore no warpaint. They were dressed much like the four mountain men and sat bareback astride their spotted ponies. Only a few had rifles; the rest carried quivers filled with decorated arrows. Bows were slung over their shoulders. Dark eyes watched the four mountain men with expressions ranging from curiosity to outright hostility.

Several moments passed before the Crow leader spoke. James translated.

"He says they were promised guns. They want these," James stated.

"Ask him, if we give them the rifles, will they allow us passage through their land?" Micah suggested. "And this too. Ask him if they took the wagon train's stock."

The hunter signed Micah's question.

A flurry of conversation passed between the braves.

"What are they saying?" hissed Packy out of the corner of his mouth.

"They're discussing our option."

"Harumph."

Long seconds passed before the chief spoke again.

Again, James translated. "He says they sold the stock

and they will allow passage. And they want Curtright."

Johan chuckled, "Ya, serves that sidewinder right."

"Ask him who he sold the stock to?"

The French-Canadian signed and the chief replied.

Lavanier turned to Cunningham and said. "Lakota."

Nodding, Micah said, "Tell them it's a deal."

Giving the crow that message, the four turned and began walking back to the overturned freight hauler and the anxious settlers.

Blood curdling yells pierced the air, causing the women to scream and clutch their children close. They all thought they were going to die.

James hissed, "Keep walking. That Crow just wants to make coup."

Thundering hooves drew closer. The leader touched Micah on the shoulder and then spun his mount away. He uttered yips of joy as he returned to the rest of the band. He was greeted by more raucous cheers and celebration.

The exchange was made quickly and without incident. Lastly, it came time to handing over the trussed-up wagon master.

Several Crow yanked the man to his feet. Curtright protested mightily. They ignored his struggles and cursing.

"You ain't got no right to let them take me!" he challenged.

"We don't? Seems your greed put a lot of innocent folks in danger."

"I did not!" he argued. "I was gonna give them their guns!"

"Yeah? When? After they killed off these settlers?" Micah asked.

Curtright spluttered, trying to form words that wouldn't come.

Svenson mockingly saluted the man as he was hauled away by the warriors.

Enraged, Curtright let fly with a wad of spit aimed at the burly Swede.

Johan swiftly dodged the spittle and grinned.

Realizing the day was half gone, Micah conferred with his comrades and then gave the order to circle the wagons.

"Come back here and get the rest of these supplies," he said. "Split them between y'all. We'll rest here and start fresh in the morning."

Relieved they had avoided certain death, the settlers chattered joyfully and hurried to do as they were told.

CHAPTER

Elizabeth Livingston sat on the box seat next to Willis Thigpen. Her two daughters, Marah and Colleen, were walking with JP alongside the schooner. They were making good time since the incident with the Crow hunting party, and the four trappers took charge of the wagon train.

"Thank you, Mr. Thigpen, for taking my daughters and me in," she said, smiling meekly at him. As she smoothed the wrinkles from her blue dress, she added, "I really had no inkling of what to do after Byron was killed and our wagon burned."

Cutting a quick glance to his passenger, Thigpen refocused on guiding the four-up and said, "We've still got a long haul, Mrs. Livingston. We are all in this together. I trust them four mountain men more than I ever trusted Curtright. They will see to it we make it to Fort Hall."

"Safely, I hope," she added.

"Oh, absolutely, Mrs. Livingston. For sure."

A huge sigh escaped his passenger's lips, and she began speaking softly as raw emotion flowed from her heart. Her words were filled with the anguish of losing a man she dearly loved.

"My husband was a good man, Mr. Thigpen," she said.

"I have no doubt of that, Mrs. Livingston," he replied, keeping his focus on the rolling plain ahead.

"He was the only blacksmith for miles around, but he was also an impatient man. The lure of what was just around the bend filled his thoughts and fueled his dreams," she continued.

"I can understand that. After my wife died of the fever, there was nothing to hold me and JP on our little farm. So, we hopped a riverboat in Cincinnati and traveled to Saint Joe. We also wanted to see what laid around the bend."

He paused to look at her and saw the proud defiance in her face. Then, he continued, "None of us know what to expect or whether we will all make it there. But if God's willing and his grace shines upon us, we all will reach this 'promised land' and thrive. That's what I hope, at least."

"You a religious man, Mr. Thigpen?"

"Well, let's just say I know who butters my bread and I thank Him every day for those blessings," Thigpen stated.

She sighed again and said, "I know. I feel it, too. His blessings, I mean. I just wish Byron could have realized his dreams."

Moisture rose in her hazel eyes. Her husband's death was still fresh in her mind. She blamed herself for his sudden passing.

Being farmers, the Livingstons knew nothing of warfare, let alone the tactics of the Indians who roamed the plains they were crossing. When the wagon train was attacked, all the couple wanted to do was protect their girls and survive. They fired their rifles randomly.

Both were in the process of reloading when one of the hostiles leaped over the tongue of their wagon and went for Elizabeth with a tomahawk poised to strike. When she screamed, her husband dropped his unloaded rifle and sprung to her defense.

Both men toppled to the ground and grappled for superiority. Her husband was no match for the younger and more powerful savage, though.

As the two fought, Elizabeth struggled to reload. She pointed and pulled the trigger just as the Indian's weapon was buried in her husband's forehead. Both men died seconds apart, a second Elizabeth wished she had back.

It was an image that would haunt her forever. Elizabeth blinked rapidly to keep the horrible memory at bay, but it did no good. Tears fell making splotches on her dress, she hastily swiped the wetness from her cheeks.

Switching the reins to one hand, Willis patted her forearm. "Don't ever lose the memories of your husband, Mrs. Livingston. Keep them close. Time is a great healer."

Sniffling, Elizabeth nodded and said, "But some days

it's just so hard."

"Yes ma'am, but your daughters need to see your inner strength; it will give them strength."

Digging a hanky from the cuff of her sleeve, Mrs. Livingston delicately blew her nose.

"You're a fine figure of a woman, Mrs. Livingston. Any man would be proud to call you his wife."

Her mouth dropped open with surprise. "I'll not marry again, Mr. Thigpen," she replied flatly.

"Yes, I said the same thing. But God has a plan for all of us. We just have to wait to see what he reveals."

Their attention was diverted when they saw Packy race past on his white mule.

"Wonder what's got him riding so hard?" Thigpen asked.

Looking around the canvas back at the string of wagons, Elizabeth said, "He's stopping to talk to Mr. Cunningham."

"Hope it's good news and not bad," Willis said.

Focusing on her daughters and JP, she said, "Children, when we reach a resting point, we need to gather buffalo chips to fuel our fire tonight."

"Yes ma'am," the three replied in unison.

Straightening in her seat, Elizabeth smiled.

"What's your hurry, Packy?" Lavanier asked when the rangy woodsman reined around and began walking his mule beside Micah, James, and Johan, who were riding drag and keeping watch over their backtrail.

"Nothin'! Just wanted to air out this ol' crowbait," Packy replied, squinting at his three friends. "I did see something interesting, though."

"Ya, like what?" Micah asked.

"Didn't that Crow chief tell us he sold the stock to some Lakota?"

Three sets of ears perked up. The men stared at Woods.

"These people had cows, goats, sheep, extra horses and such stolen, right?"

"Ya," answered Johan.

"Well, I found 'em."

"You was supposed to be looking for the buff."

"They was up there too, still traveling west," Packy said.

"Did you find our old campsite?"

"Yep, stayed there one night 'fore I came looking fer y'all."

"How far are we from that?" Micah asked.

"Get there by nightfall," Packy stated.

"And this stock you found?"

"Not far from there."

"And?" James said, growing impatient.

"And it looks to be a different hunting party than them Crow we run into back yonder."

"Who?"

"Couldn't tell. Kept my distance," Woods said and fanned himself with his hat.

"All right," James began. "Go guide Thigpen to our old base camp. We'll set up there for the night."

Packy urged the mule into an uneven trot toward the Thigpen wagon.

"Might be able to get these folks stock back for 'em," Micah said with a toothy grin.

"Or stir up a hornet's nest," added James.

"Ya, that too," chuckled Johan.

CHAPTER 9

"More coffee, Mr. Cunningham?" Elizabeth Livingston asked as they all sat around a large campfire..

"Thankee kindly, ma'am," he replied, holding out his cup.

She filled and asked, "How's your arm?"

He nodded to her and said, "It's fine ma'am. Thank you for bandaging it."

"You are more than welcome, Mr. Cunningham." Then, she turned and made the rounds of the others who were relaxing around the fire.

That gave Micah the time to study her. She was a handsome woman. Medium height and lean. She wore her dark hair in a loose bun at the nape of her neck, the fly-away stands framing her face and hazel eyes. If he were of the mind to take a woman, her kind would be his choice. He wasn't, though. Nonetheless, she was just a bit too genteel for his taste. He slurped another sip of coffee. A good squaw was more to his liking. He smiled inwardly, his ears retuning to the conversation around the fire.

"You really think you could get our stock back?" JP asked with eyes wide.

"Gonna try, son," Lavanier replied.

The youngster actually looked excited. He turned to his father and said, "Golly, wouldn't that be somethin', Pa?"

"It would, son. It would," Willis replied.

"Fresh milk would be nice to have again," chimed in Mrs. Livingston.

Hoofbeats rung out from behind the wagon, prompting a display of rifles as James and Micah each took position at front and back. They peered around its sides and waited.

Svenson gave each a squirrely look as he reined up the bay he was riding and slid to the ground.

"You two spooked now?" he asked, wrapping the reins around the metal rimmed wheel.

With hands on his hips, his eyes narrowed as he gauged their expressions. Finally, he nodded and said, "Ya, you two is spooked."

He stepped around them, cradling the short barrel Hawken. Cunningham grabbed him by the arm and asked, "What did you find?"

The Swede shrugged his wide shoulders and said, "Not much." He walked around the wagon, poured himself a cup of coffee and took a healthy sip before continuing. "Looks like they're tucked in for the night. Brought their squaws with them; kids too. It looks they are here for the season."

"How much stock are we talking about?" James asked.

"Twenty head maybe."

Scanning the inside of the small circle, Micah announced, "It's too small in here for that amount of stock. We'll have to put them outside and place guards; if we want to keep them."

Thigpen stepped forward. "Are you saying the Crow took our stock and sold them? So, now we are dealing with some other tribe?"

"Seems that way." Micah explained. "Some of these tribes barter back and forth with each other."

Thigpen's jaw dropped in surprise.

Cunningham grinned, "White men do the same, don't they?"

Scratching his head, Thigpen nodded saying, "Yeah, I guess so."

Looking at the sky, Micah added, "We'll go pay 'em a visit in an hour or so. We'll wait 'til it's good and dark. In the meantime, Willis, why don't you tell me about the rest of the families in this train?"

Thigpen looked up and pointed to one wagon. "That's the Underhills, a family of five. Came from Pennsylvania. Tic Underhill is a troublemaker."

His finger moved to the next wagon and he added,.

"The Bailey couple are newlyweds from Ohio, same as me and my son."

He went on to name the other seven families. He looked at the trappers and continued, "As a whole, we're good people with an urge to better ourselves. We all want to see what is out here in this frontier territory."

"Ya, they good people as long as they stand and fight," Johan replied.

"I admit, we are a little green," Thigpen remarked. "But with you four — all experienced men — at our side, we're better. You just lead and guide us. We'll stand up to protect ourselves and our stock."

The hunters cut each other a look, then James said, "We'll need everyone capable of firing a rifle to be ready. Even the women and any of the young'uns old enough to load and handle a weapon."

"We'll be ready," acknowledged Thigpen.

"Good."

Slithering through the wet grasses, the woodsmen eased closer to the stolen stock. Parting the tall blades for a better look, they lay silent and studied the situation. Their ears were perked for the slightest noise out of the ordinary. All eyes were alert and noses took in the scent of dampness, fresh prairie grass and chip fires. Stillness surrounded them.

"I don't see any braves guarding the stock," Micah declared.

Whispering, James chimed in, "They must be mighty comfortable to do that."

"Ya, they don't know about us yet," added Johan.

"That will change, if we can't get the stock away from them without a ruckus."

The men lapsed into silence, thinking hard on the best way to retrieve the animals.

"Well boys, what do ya say?"

Turning on his side. Micah grinned, "I say we mount up and drive this herd home."

"Amen."

"Ya, and get ready to fight," the Swede added.

"Ain't that the dad-blamed truth," added Packy.

Circling the stolen herd, the men moved as quietly as they could without spooking the animals. Slowly but surely, they began pushing the stock toward the wagon train.

Bleating, bawling and nickers kept the four looking over their shoulders for an uprising. They knew the sounds would carry in the quiet of the night.

Packy's mule didn't understand what he was supposed

to do and bucked a few times, startling the cows nearby.

"Here now, ya ornery cuss," he argued, trying to keep his voice low, kicking the animal in the ribs. "Settle down!"

Riding close, Micah whispered "Get that damn jackass under control 'fore ya spook the whole herd, Packy."

The lanky woodsman glared at him and hissed right back, "Shad-up, Cunningham!"

Micah grinned and looked over his shoulder toward the Indian camp. It was out of their view now, but he didn't relax. A charge could come at any moment. Nudging his roan next to the white mule. he whispered, "Go back and keep an eye on the camp."

Packy frowned, "Why me? How 'bout you."

"Cause that damn mule of yours is a problem."

"Well, he ain't been trained to herd cows," the ornery trapper said.

"Just do it, will ya?"

Giving his friend a dirty look, Packy reluctantly turned and headed back in the direction they had just left.

Keeping the herd contained was a challenge, especially in the dark. Cows wandered off every which way. The sheep bleated like they were blindly lost. Only the horses seemed to keep a nice pace in the lead. Finally, the cows and sheep fell into step behind the horses, minimizing the amount of time the woodsmen had to chase strays.

Sitting astride his mule and resting his forearm on the saddle horn, Packy kept his eyes peeled on the Indian camp. His mule ripping and chewing the lush grasses beneath him was the only sound he heard. He was out of sight, behind a rocky escarpment.

A slim line of color began gracing the eastern sky with the diminishing stars overhead as a backdrop. He could smell the heavy dew mixing slightly with the smoldering smoke from the Lakota fires. The wind was calm for the time being. Later it would pick up and blow as it always did on the plains.

Squinting, he detected movement. Squaws scurried out of their teepees to tend morning fires and readying for the day.

Packy sat up straighter when two braves emerged from teepees in the back. His eyes were glued to them. They moseyed to the front of the camp and looked his way. The hairs on the back of his neck tingled.

One pointed.

The other gestured, slapping at the first one's hand. A short conversation ensued, and one of them walked off toward one of the fires. The other struck off to where the herd had been.

Packy sipped air.

With the sky getting lighter, the trapper slipped out of the saddle and dropped to the ground, parting the grasses to follow the braves' approach. The hairs on the back of his neck tingled some more.

He waited and watched.

Reaching the spot where the herd had once grazed, the redskin paused. He studied the ground and let his eyes scan the area. Whirling, he ran back to the camp.

The huntsman could hear the guttural words coming from brave's mouth as he alerted the encampment of the stolen animals. Indians stumbled from their teepees and swarmed the messenger, who now was gesturing wildly and pointing.

"Well now, time to go," whispered Packy.

He pushed himself off the ground and mounted. He whirled and spurred the dingy-colored mule into a run.

Guided by three trappers, the herd arrived at its destination alongside the wagon train. The bawling and bleating roused the settlers, who walked out of the safety of the circle to watch their cattle being returned.

Excited conversation drifted among the travelers. Feet danced little jigs as boisterous voices celebrated and the pioneers exchanged hugs.

The sun's early rays made the grasses sparkle like diamonds. Relief again overwhelmed the settlers. The mountain men from Sinking Springs had further entrenched themselves within the hearts of these tired and bedraggled pioneers.

Hearing hooves pummel the thick turf, James hitched around in his saddle. Packy was heading at them in a full run.

Alerting his comrades, James shouted, "Here comes that skinny hide hunter."

The trappers' heads swung, features breaking into a grin. Eyes narrowed with apprehension because of the speed with which their friend was approaching.

"That don't look good," mumbled Johan.

Micah agreed, "Nope."

Packy reined the mule to an abrupt stop, causing the animal to hack and heave for air. Taking a deep breath for his own deflated lungs, Packy rasped a simple warning, "Better get ready. Them redskins saw the herd was gone. They'll be coming soon."

Silence reigned between the four, each with their own thoughts. The joyful settlers still were celebrating, unaware of the danger lurking a few moments away.

Four sets of eyes connected. Without a word, they nodded in unison.

James raised his voice to the gleeful travelers. "Go

back to camp. Dig out every weapon you have."

Confused, the settlers peppered the air with questions: "What? Why? What are you talking about? We need to milk some of these cows."

Johan bellowed, "Quiet!"

The chatter simmered.

"Get back to the wagons. Them redskins is on their way to take back your cattle."

"Prepare for a fight," Micah shouted. When he saw them hesitate, he added, "That's an order!"

Nervously, Elizabeth clutched Willis' arm in a death grip. "Mr. Thigpen?"

"Just do as they say," he said as he grabbed her by the elbow and guided her back to the wagon. "Do you know how to pack a rifle?"

Numbly, she nodded and said, "I can shoot, too."

"Good. How about your daughters?"

"Marah can. She's more of a tomboy than Colleen."

"Good. We'll be ready," Willis instructed.

James announced, "I hid some of them Hawken rifles from the Crow, along with shot and a few kegs of powder. Put them in Thigpen's wagon."

"Good, we'll need 'em," Micah replied. Turning to Packy, he added, "Go hand out those spare rifles to those who need one."

Finally, he returned his gaze to Johan and James. "Let's go fortify where we can," he said. "It won't take long for them Indians to get here."

CHAPTER  10

A quiet swept over the wagon train as fear touched every heart. Adrenalin was running high. Breathing was rapid. More than one defender wondered if soon they would meet their Maker. Sweaty palms sought relief against shirts, britches and aprons.

A baby squalled on the other side of the circle breaking the silence. Every head turned toward the sound, then back to the horizon.

They waited.

James elbowed Svenson when he spotted movement on the ridge, jerking his head in that direction.

Johan nodded and jabbed Micah's arm. He silently passed the word along.

"I see 'em," he said as his eyes flicked around the encampment. "I'll go alert the settlers. They need to keep their shirts on and hold their fire until they see they are in range. We can't afford to waste ammunition," he grinned.

Snorting, Packy said, "Let's hope they can hit what they aim at."

Chuckling, the Swede added, "Ya, for sure that."

"Make sure they know it's important to conserve lead when they can," James added.

Approaching the first wagon, Micah scanned the weapons leaning against the side of schooner. He immediately asked, "Those loaded?"

The couple nodded. Fear laced their eyes, but their mouths were set in a determined line.

"Can you hit what you aim at?"

The two threw a quick glance at each other and replied confidently, "Yes."

"Good. We don't have powder and lead to waste. Wait 'til you have a good shot before firing."

"Aye."

Turning, Cunningham moved to the next wagon. He checked their weapons and offered the same advice before continuing on to the Thigpen wagon.

After listening to Micah, Willis asked, "How's the rest of the folks?"

Thinking about the man's words and not wanting to implicate anyone, he mustered an answer. "Passable, but one never knows how a shavetail will react under pressure," he said.

Thigpen pulled his short stature taller and stated, "That might be so, Mr. Cunningham, but we are a hardy stock. We don't give up easily or we never would have made this trek."

Micah's eyes narrowed. The man's defiance was commendable. He paused and added, "I surely hope you are right, Mr. Thigpen. I really do." Then, he walked away.

"They ready?" James asked when Micah returned..

The woodsman shrugged and said, "For the most part. Time will tell."

"Got a hell of a lot a greenhorns on this train." Packy declared. "They's gonna find out right quick this ain't no Sunday picnic."

"They learn," the big Swede chimed in. "Didn't fare too bad the last time."

"Every attack is different," Lavanier explained. "Until ya live with 'em and knows their ways, a regular white man ain't savvy ta that. Them reds'll be fightin' with everything they got."

Micah said, "I think we need to split up and keep these folks from shooting too soon. When the redskins get close, it's best we tell them when to fire."

Agreement was instantaneous. The seasoned fighters broke up and headed in four different directions. The veterans stationed themselves among the pioneers and waited for the dreaded onslaught.

War hoops pierced the air, as warriors descended upon the vulnerable train.

Packy hollered, "Hold your fire!"

The others picked up his call and it echoed down the line.

Rifles were positioned between the spokes of the wheels, around the edges of the schooners and from any position that would provide protection and a clear shot. The settlers hunkered down. They were ready.

Hearts rattled against ribs. Breathing accelerated. Eyes squinted or grew round with fear. Children squalled for attention until hands covered their mouths.

JP watched it all with wide-eyed amazement. Inching closer he asked, "Mr. Cunningham, why are their ponies painted?"

Without looking at the kid, Micah whispered, "They're going to war."

"Against us?"

"Yes."

"Just because we took our cattle back?"

"Yes."

The conversation was aborted when the call to "Fire!" went out and echoed through the encampment. Rifles and pistol muzzles spat flames. The reports echoed across the rolling plains.

Braves spun off the backs of their mounts.

The sound of arrows striking the wooden sides of the wagons, strengthened the defenders' resolve. Hot lead filled the air. Women and older children reloaded as fast as they could.

More redskins fell as did a few of the homesteaders. Their screams mingled with the raw yips and blood-curdling shrieks of the attackers. The noise was deafening.

Thigpen yelled and fell forward onto the turf, an arrow stuck in his back.

"Pa!" yelled JP.

Elizabeth screamed "No!" She dropped the rifle she was loading and rushed to Willis' side.

Micah whirled. Handing his rifle to a wide-eyed Marah and ordered her to reload. Jumping to Thigpen's aid, he placed a knee on his back and warned, "This is gonna smart."

He looked quickly to Mrs. Livingston and ordered, "Hold him down. Put all your weight on his shoulders." Then he looked for the boy and said, "Son, sit on his legs."

"Yes sir!"

Wrapping his hand around the arrow's shaft, Micah asked, "You ready, Thigpen?"

The stocky defender nodded and squeezed his eyes

shut. Cunningham took a deep breath and exhaled. Then, he gripped the arrow tightly.

Thigpen screamed.

Terror reigned across Elizabeth's face as she stared at the woodsman.

"Hang on, Thigpen. One more pull should do it," Micah said with clenched teeth. He readjusted his grip, gave another yank and the arrow exited the man's back.

A guttural cry came from the Ohioan before he fell silent. He surrendered to the pain and passed out.

Micah smiled grimly at Elizabeth and said, "He'll live."

He immediately noticed her eyes widen and her mouth drop, a warning of danger. Micah ducked and rolled, then leaped to his feet. Bowie in hand, he dove at the brave who had penetrated their perimeter. The knife buried deep into his torso and Micah pulled upward against his rib cage. Blood gushed and drenched Micah's fist as the renegade collapsed and died at his feet.

His eyes darted quickly around the camp. The battle had turned to hand-to-hand combat. He issued orders, "Load the rifles and shoot!"

"But Willis needs…" Elizabeth protested.

"Do it, now!"

Reluctantly she rose and scrambled to do as told.

Turning, Cunningham leaped into the fray. Tackling redskin after redskin. Driving the blade home each time, then pulling it out to charge another. His peripheral vision saw nothing but a whirl of bodies. His mind singularly focused on each opponent.

Lavanier battered one brave, gutted another and ran smack-dab into Micah.

Both men threw a surprised glance at each other before turning and standing back-to-back. The struggle continued.

Taking a quick breath, Cunningham looked for Svenson and Woods. They were still standing.

As abruptly as the fight began, it ended. Only a few renegades survived. The rest jumped astride their horses and rode off.

Breathless, the four woodsmen came together in the center of the camp, chests heaving and lungs burning.

Finally, Packy squeaked, "Well, that was a nice little dance."

Wiping his bloody Bowie across his leather britches, the Swede sucked air into his deflated lungs and said, "Ya, that sure cleared the cobwebs."

James nodded toward the settlers and said, "Let's see what kinda damage we got."

"Check to see if we still got stock, too. We need to get everyone patched up, bury the dead and move out again when it gets dark," added Micah. "We're sitting ducks out here."

"Aye, good idea."

CHAPTER  11

Under the moon's halo, ten wagons crawled through the night. The blackness seemed splintered by the millions of stars shedding weak light upon the lone caravan.

Not a soul whispered. All were worn out from the physical, mental and emotional strain they had been under the last twenty-four hours. A war now raged within their bodies; they craved rest but had to keep moving.

Packy drove the Bailey wagon, his dingy white mule trailing placidly behind. The young newlyweds perished in the attack. The wife's skull had been split by a tomahawk and her husband's throat slit. They were buried together.

The stock had been gathered. JP and a few of the older boys ramrodded the herd, keeping pace alongside the wagons.

The train was lucky. The Bailey's were the only two who had died during the onslaught. Another ten were wounded. leaving a sparse few to man rifles and defend the others should another attack materialize.

The heroic mountain men knew they had to remain on

the move to keep the hardy travelers safe.

The pioneers no longer eyed their adventure to a new land through rose-colored glasses. Their bright dreams of a "promised land" had been shattered. Now, they fought for survival, second by second, hour by hour, day by day.

James and the Swede were riding with the Thigpen wagon, when Micah rode up.

"Might be good to let these folks take a breather," he suggested and squinted at the horizon, "Got a few more hours before daylight."

Driving Willis' wagon, Mrs. Livingston's ears tried to focus on the conversation between the three men, but the squeaking wheels and the rattling of things in the back made it impossible.

"These wagons is slower than cold molasses," remarked Johan.

Nodding toward the direction they were headed, James asked, "What's ahead?"

Keeping his roan at a walk, Micah answered, "About seven miles ahead there's fresh buff sign and a stand of pine and cottonwoods. They could give us protection if we lay over for a few days. We could let the settlers rest up there and tend the wounded, instead of stopping here. Figured we could hunt some buffalo and stock these folks up with meat. Antelope too. There's also fresh water ahead."

"Sounds like heaven," James added. A toothy grin

filled his stubbled ebony face.

Hitching around in his saddle Micah gazed at the wagons that trailed behind and said, "To these folks, it would be just that, I reckon."

"Ya, let's keep going. Rest when we get there." Johan said.

Elizabeth let a whoosh of air escape hearing the news. She was about done in. Glancing over her shoulder into the wagon bed, she could just make out the forms of her sleeping daughters and Mr. Thigpen. She refocused on the team, praying she could hold out for just a few more hours.

"Sounds good," Micah said and whirled the roan around so he could inform Packy of the plan.

Micah repeated his plan for the lanky woodsman.

"We'll continue for a couple more hours. Found us a nice place to camp for a few days. Hunt some buff and antelope," he said.

"About time. My arse is worn clear down to the bone sitting on this hard seat," he complained.

You ain't been sitting there more'n a few hours."

"A few hours too long if ya ask me."

"You just don't have padding in the right places is your problem. Mrs. Livingston ain't complained a lick," he said and grinned.

Woods shot him a venomous look.

"Ya need to eat more, old pard," Micah said and chuckled. He knew full well Packy could devour as much food as the three of them in one sitting. Where he put it, no one knew. The tall drink of water seemed to burn food as fast as he ate it.

Packy ignored him and refocused on the teams. As Micah rode off, he mumbled, "Like ta see one of yins sit on this hard seat for hours at a time, ya old scudder."

Through the years, Woods had fine-tuned his hearing in the wilds of the Rocky Mountains. He could pick out the death rattle of an oak leaf as winter approached. The crunch of grass under hooves or padded feet clamored loud to him. He never missed the swish of a rattler slithering through crevasses or underbrush.

Now, above the jangling coming from inside the schooner and wheels squeaking, he heard something. Shifting the reins of the four-up to his left hand, he scooted to the right and peered around the torn and loose bonnet that flapped uncontrollably with the jostling of the wagon.

On the eastern horizon a yellow-orange ball was presenting itself. Rays of light poked through the sky interlacing with leaded clouds. That ball would soon disappear leaving nothing but a thick gray covering.

Packy snorted, not liking what he saw. His nose already was picking up the scent of rain.

Shrugging off the likelihood of a monsoon, he turned his attention back to that itchy feeling he had that something or someone was afoot.

A line of black silhouettes came into view as the sun climbed. Packy's eyes narrowed and he swore softly, "Dammit!"

He pondered the situation but didn't take his eyes of the warriors, expecting movement. He couldn't tell if they were the same Indians from the earlier attack or a new tribe hell-bent on bushwhacking the near defenseless homesteaders. Some of the Plains Indians attacked for the pure enjoyment of killing and stealing.

"Someone's got their breechcloths all in a twist!" he whispered to himself. He knew hunting parties normally didn't go on rampages unless provoked. He cursed the situation they all were in.

Damn you, Curtright, for stirring up trouble for these settlers.

His head swiveled, gazing up the line. The dim light showcasing the vulnerability of the caravan, strung out and moving slow.

Abruptly he slid across the seat and readjusted the reins of the four-up in his hands. Slapping rumps, he moved them out of the rear of the line and urged them into a lope.

Passing James, he yelled, thumbing over his shoulder, "Got trouble! Whip 'em up and pray we reach them trees in time!"

Surprised, Lavanier rounded to scan the eastern horizon. The braves were still in silhouette but now moving in their direction. He could hear Packy sending the alarm up the line. The wagons' mules and horses picked up their pace.

Horses snorted at the abrupt change of tempo. Hooves began to pound the turf, as fear once again filled the eyes of man and animal.

James pointed to the advancing renegades. Johan looked and asked, "What do you think they want?"

"Who knows," returned James.

Cunningham hitched around in his saddle to study the situation. The wagons were moving at a brisk pace, but he was worried.

"Those folks are as tired as their stock. Might not make it to cover in time," he said.

"Johan, fire up them kids! Get that herd moving!" he called out.

"Risking a stampede, ain't ya?" Johan said.

"Maybe but we need 'em."

Johan nodded and bolted toward the remuda.

James also looked to the west and asked, "How much farther?"

"Couple of miles," Micah replied.

In unison, both men gazed to the east.

"The wagons won't make it in time if those braves decide to have a hissy fit."

James chuckled at Micah's choice of words.

Cunningham grinned at the French-Canadian and suggested, "How 'bout we play a little cat and mouse?"

Lavanier knew immediately what his partner had in mind and asked, "How far ya wanna go?"

The devious woodsman took off his hat, scratched above his ear and said, "Far enough for these folks to get to the trees."

Nodding slightly and slapping the ratty felt back on his head, the two of them rammed heels into their horses' ribs. Their mounts grunted in surprise and charged hard toward the Indians.

Brandishing their rifles over their heads, the men yipped, hooted and hollered at the braves making the redskins pull up abruptly. Their arms waved wildly, pointing and chattering while watching the display put on by the two buckskin-clad men.

Twenty yards from the party, Micah and James swerved their horses hopefully taking the Indians with them away from the homesteaders.

Raising a lance, their leader shouted orders.

The line broke and gave chase, yelling and screeching

in pursuit.

Flashing a grin at James, Micah yelled, "Let 'er rip, man!"

Hearing the commotion behind them, Packy didn't even bother to look back. He ran his wagon alongside the Thigpen schooner and shouted, "Follow me!"

Face pale and fraught with tension and fear, Elizabeth Livingston didn't know if she had the strength to manage the horses at a dead run.

"Whip 'em up, Mrs. Livingston! Whip 'em up!" Packy urged as the two teams raced forward.

Elizabeth took a deep breath and pulled strength from depths she was unaware existed. She screeched at the team, "Ya! Ya!" Sliding the reins into her left hand she pulled the whip from a side pocket and snapped it over their heads, prompting a burst of speed from the animals.

Inside the wagon, fear plastered the girls' faces as they gripped the sideboards to keep from being tossed every which way.

In immense pain, Thigpen struggled to sit up and move toward the tailgate. When he reached it, he hauled in air and rested for a few moments. The pain was sucking the life out of him. His eyes squinted at the two girls as he called out, "Hand me a rifle!"

Colleen couldn't move. Fear handcuffed her body, holding her prisoner. Her eyes darted back to Thigpen and then to Marah. She'd never seen her mother act so as she yelled and whipped the team. Her body shivered uncontrollably. Her teeth chattered as she brought her gaze back to Thigpen.

Grunting, Marah tried to reach the rifles buried under items that had toppled during the run. Finally, her hand touched cold metal. Wrapping both hands around one rifle barrel, she pulled. It moved a tad.

Taking a deep breath and re-adjusting her grip, Marah tugged again, but couldn't free the carbine.

"Help your sister," Thigpen ordered..

Her mouth opened, but no words would come.

"Do it!" he shouted.

Colleen didn't budge.

Realizing the child was frozen with fear, Thigpen knew it was no use to yell; it would just frighten her more. His gaze flicked to Marah and he calmly stated, "I can't help you child. You will have to dig the rifle out yourself."

Marah nodded slightly and refocused. Sitting back on her knees, she studied the way the load had shifted as the schooner raced over uneven ground. She pushed and shoved items out of the way until she could pull the rifle free.

Finally, succeeding, Marah turned and handed the Hawken to Thigpen.

Taking it, he asked, "Is it loaded?"

Marah frowned and replied, "Of course it is. I loaded it myself."

A faint smile touched his pale face at the girl's spunk. "Good, girl," he said and turned his attention to landscape behind them. The jostling became worse. The three in the back could barely sit upright.

"Elizabeth! What the hell are you doing?" yelled Thigpen.

Her arms and fingers had gone numb as she encouraged the team's mad dash to safety. Struggling with controlling the team, she paid no attention to what was happening behind her.

CHAPTER  12

Reaching the safety of the trees, Packy drove deeper into the tall cover. The team hacked, wheezed, and coughed as they strained to pull air into their emptied lungs. Woods did, too. Disregarding the lathered horses, he wrapped the reins around the brake and stiffly climbed down from the seat. Stretching and popping his limbs, he gazed back to see others pulling under the cover. He counted the wagons as they arrived. Doing a doubletake, he counted again. One of the wagons was missing. Quickly scanning the plains, he saw the Thigpen wagon careening off in another direction.

He issued clipped orders. "Y'all get ready to make a stand!" he yelled. Then, he ran to his mule, ripped the tethered reins free and scrambled into the saddle. Slamming heels to ribs, he booted the mule toward the runaway wagon.

Thigpen knew something was wrong. He struggled to crawl to the seat at the front amidst the bouncing and jostling. The pain from his wound was making his eyes water. He knew Elizabeth needed help.

Time abruptly ran out. Thigpen felt the wheels on his

left leave the ground tilting the bed.

The kingpin snapped, releasing the doubletree from the base of the wagon. It jarred the horses and caused them to explode into a burst of speed.

Elizabeth screamed when the reins zipped through her fingers.

Marah and Colleen squealed in fright trying to reach their mother.

Packy watched in wide-eyed disbelief as the wagon flipped onto its side and continued to skid, finally coming to a stop on the opposite side.

"Aw, hell!" he muttered, whipping the mule with the reins, pushing it to the limit.

Riding upon the disaster, he flew out of the saddle, praying he would find survivors.

Cunningham trailed Lavanier by a length, casting looks over his shoulder keeping an eye on the redskins.

Tossing a glance at Micah, James let fly with a big grin and turned his focus to where they would go next.

They zipped and zagged over open ground and took a few turns through scattered trees. They were determined to lure the party away from the wagon train, and it was working.

The warriors behind them had split into three groups. Two were on each flank of the woodsmen. The third remained behind them.

"We got company!" the Frenchman shouted and pointed. "Buffalo!"

Both horses swerved in rhythm toward the massive herd. It was the best way to shake the unwavering pursuit of the warriors.

Without uttering a word, Micah and James separated. Instinctively, they rode to the far ends of the herd. Their plan was to spook the buffalo into a stampede toward the Indians.

Rounding the outer edges, they began yelling and waving their hats at the burly, curly-haired mammoths. The shaggy beasts were in no hurry to move though.

So, Micah reined up the roan, pulled the Hawken from its boot and fired over the animal's heads. James mimicked the motion.

The boom of the .50 caliber rifles made heads pop up from their feeding. A few turned abruptly and spooked others. The pace picked up and the herd began to race toward the warriors.

The ground shook, and thunder rolled across the ground as if it came from the heavens.

Micah slanted a look at James and grinned.

Both watched as the big herd moved as one large brown mass, dust flying from thousands of hooves hitting the turf.

The warriors slid to a stop, stunned for a few moments trying to digest the situation. When it dawned on them, they whirled their mounts and skedaddled.

Resting with forearms on saddle horns, the woodsmen watched the bedlam ensue as the herd stampeded east.

"Think that will keep 'em busy fer a while," Micah commented.

"For sure," chimed in James.

Johan Svenson, JP Thigpen and few others had reached the shelter of the trees with the trains' stock.

Stepping out of the leather, Johan surveyed the scene. Teams had been unhitched and hobbled. After the long haul, they were enjoying a feeding frenzy.

The chatter from the settlers was light but mindful of the pending danger. Rifles were leaning against sideboards, ready for an attack. Svenson looked over his shoulder to the prairie below, hoping to spot James and Micah..

JP rode through the settlers looking for the Thigpen wagon. He frowned and was puzzled when he couldn't find it. He inquired at the nearest wagon.

"Mrs. Henderson? Know where my Pa's wagon is?"

Stepping over the tongue, Mr. Henderson spoke before

his wife could answer. "Saw the wagon veer off. Then that skinny hide-hunter hopped his mule and took off after them," he said.

JP's face blanched. He whirled his horse and rode toward the burly Swede, yelling, "Mr. Svenson! Mr. Svenson!"

Johan spun when he heard the anguished cry.

"Mr. Svenson! Something is wrong!" JP stated excitedly.

Grabbing the bridle of the boy's horse, he spoke calmly, "Easy, son! Easy now!"

JP spewed the words out in a flurry. "My Pa's wagon ain't here. Mr. Henderson said it veered off and Mr. Woods hightailed after it," he said, gasping for air.

Stepping back into the saddle, the Swede asked, "What direction?"

JP pointed and proclaimed, "Somewhere out there."

Must have been a runaway wagon,

"Let's go, son," he ordered.

"Yes sir."

When they arrived at the crash scene, they spotted Woods' mule off to the side, but Packy wasn't anywhere to be seen.

Seeing the wreckage, JP screamed, "Pa!" and left the Swede in his wake.

Johan let loose with a low whistle. Contents were scattered hither and yon. The bonnet was crushed, the bows splintered. Wheels were smoking and still spinning to the point sparks could ignite any second.

He hollered, "Packy!"

A faint voice rose in the air.

"Over here," came a short reply.

Dismounting and ground-tying his horse, Johan rounded the wagon bed. What he saw made him mutter under his breath, "Dammit all ta hell!"

The boy was cradling his father, tears leaving white streaks through the dirt caked skin. Two girls lay not far away aside their mother.

Packy looked up. "Need you to help me lift this wagon up."

Putting his God-given strength to use, the Swede's muscles bulged under the buckskin shirt. Somehow, he and Packy lifted the wagon off Thigpen.

"Now, boy! Pull him out," Packy shouted with grit teeth.

JP quickly pulled his father from the wreckage. Laying him down gently.

The wood thudded heavily back to the ground.

Taking a deep breath, Johan nodded toward the others, "Dead?"

Swinging his head, Packy stared at the three females. "No. By the grace of God, they's all still alive."

Letting go of the breath he had been holding, Johan walked over and squatted by the mother. He made a quick examination.

Packy followed and said, "Can't tell what got hurt, but they's all breathing, including Thigpen."

Standing again, Svenson looked around. "What happened?"

Woods led the way back to the front and pointed, "Looks ta me the pin snapped, and she must've hit every rock and hole. When's ya got a runaway team, ain't nobody — not man or woman — can control the beasts. When them animals get blindsided by fear, ain't no helpin' 'til they run out of steam."

Before he could answer, they heard hooves thundering across the turf. Both turned toward the sound. To their relief, James and Micah reined their horse to a skidding stop in front of them.

"It's 'bout time you two quit playing with them redskins and showed up," Packy groused.

"We kept them yellow dogs off your tails," James retorted.

"Anyone hurt?" Micah asked.

"Ya, all four of 'em," answered Johan.

"Thigpen and Livingston?" Micha asked.

"Ya."

"Where's JP?"

Thumbing over his shoulder, "With his Pa." Johan added. He pointed at Micah's rope, and added, "We need to flip it back right, load 'em and tend to these folks back at camp."

Both riders tossed their ropes to Johan and Packy, who in turned half-hitched the lassos to the top rims of the two wheels.

Maneuvering their horses around they managed to pull it upright.

Packy climbed up on the gate and began cutting the dismantled canvas clear. The bows were too damaged to fix as he moved them out of the way to load the injured travelers.

Tossing the canvas to Johan, "We can carry them on this, if need be," he offered.

"Son, we'll take care of your pa. You go find them horses and bring 'em back," Micah ordered.

"But…" JP countered.

"Boy, we need them horses," Micah insisted

Giving his father one last look, JP reluctantly rose and walked to his horse, picked up the reins and mounted.

Marah and Colleen were sitting next to their mother when the three walked back to them.

"You girls all right?"

Colleen still had that cornered doe look in her eye, but Marah answered, "A few bumps and bruises, but we're alive by God's grace." Her eyes drifted to Thigpen and she asked, "Is he... ah... Is he going to live?"

"Yes, he's too ornery to die, I reckon," he answered.

She exhaled loudly.

"Don't know yet how badly he was hurt. Will know more once we get him back to camp. Having that arrow wound ain't gonna make recovery easy," James' said and flicked a glance to their mother. She was lying still. Her eyes were closed and her face was the color of rice powder.

"How's your ma?" he asked.

"She said she felt like her head was gonna split open before she passed out again," the young girl replied.

Taking one knee, the French-Canadian scooped Mrs. Livingston into his arms and walked back to the wagon.

Micah and Packy had made Thigpen as comfortable as they could. Next, they picked up the thrown contents and stashed them where they could.

Packy pointed and said, "Here comes JP."

"That was quick."

"Well now boys, we's gotta figure some way ta hitch that team up again," Packy said, scratching his head in an effort to get his brain working. His eyes bounced from one to the other. "That pin snapped clear in two."

"Ya!" agreed Johan. He walked to the front and pointed out their dilemma to Micah and James.

Thunder echoed in the distance. Everyone looked to the sky. The heavy clouds were thick with rain and they could see in the distance sheets of it obscuring the ridges.

"Damn!" muttered Packy. "Don't need that right now. But on the bright side, twixt that buff herd and the rain, them redskins won't be bothering us fer a spell."

No one bothered to answer. Everyone was lost in their own thoughts.

Micah returned his focus to the pin hole, racking his brain on what they could use. Turning to JP, he said, "Son, ya got anything in this wagon of yours we might could use as a pin? Just to get us back to camp?"

"How's Pa?"

"Still out cold."

The lad nodded and slipped out of the leather. "I don't know, I'll have to look."

Rummaging around in the toolbox with Micah leaning over his shoulder, JP pulled out the nippers, holding them so close to the woodsman's face he reared back.

"Might could stick one handle in the hole, not sure if it would hold, though," JP suggested.

"A wooden peg would work better," James offered up.

Svenson peered over their shoulders.

"Ya, the rung on that chair would work," he said pointing to a busted seat.

"That's it," Cunningham replied.

Work commenced and the wagon was ready to roll as the first drops of pelting rain descended.

CHAPTER  13

Willis Thigpen was on the mend. Stock and pioneers seemed rested. Wagons, harnesses and torn bonnets were repaired, and wheels greased. Washing was done and water gathered. Meat from the hunts was salted or dried for jerky.

The settlers became restless, they knew time was running out. They became irritated because the mountain men sat on their butts, wasting daylight.

The four men kept an eye on the building unrest. They had no idea the specific month, but nature was telling them it was mid to late August, maybe later. The journey to Fort Hall was still a far piece, and most days they were lucky to make ten miles. They needed the remuda and settlers well rested and wagons fixed for the next part of the trail. That would be the hardest, wearing on even the hardiest of men and beast.

Tic Underhill had been itching to get moving two days after they reached the sheltered grove. When they didn't, he began slowly fanning the flames of discontent.

Leading a few homesteaders that included three of his sons, Tic Underhill marched into the Thigpen encampment to speak his mind.

"Tick-tock! Tick-tock! Here it comes. He's got his britches all in a twist," mumbled Packy. His words were just low enough only those seated closest could hear.

Micah and James slanted a glance at each other.

Johan leaned back against a wheel, crossed his ankles, folded his arms and grinned. He puffed energetically on his clay pipe. Smoke curled around his head before fleeing into the night air.

Thigpen was resting in a hammock tied between a tree and the wagon. Elizabeth and her girls were cleaning up after supper. JP was gathering more wood for the fire.

Sticking thumbs through his suspenders, Underhill struck a pose. Feet splayed, face hard, eyes threatening and chest puffed out like a prairie chicken during mating season, he looked confident.

"We wanna talk to you, boys," he declared, spitting the word "boys" like it was cow dung.

It did not go unnoticed by the four woodsmen.

Micah's brow rose and one eye squinted. He moved the chaw of tobacco from one cheek to another and spit a string of brown juice into the fire where it sizzled for a few seconds.

James' jaw clinched. Because of his dark skin, he had

114

been called boy more times than he could count, and never liked it.

Packy's lips thinned as he sent a doubting look at his comrades.

Johan's grin spread and he chuckled.

Thigpen struggled to sit up.

Elizabeth turned, wiped her hands on her apron, gathered her girls and backed off toward the wagon.

His arms loaded with deadfall, JP slowed his approach to the camp as he saw the confrontation unfold. By their posture he figured men were there to make trouble. Cautiously, he continued forward, dropping the wood near the fire, then moved to stand by his father. His eyes darted from one to the other, finally landing on the men from Sinking Springs. Like everyone else, he waited.

Svenson removed the pipe stem from his mouth, tapped the dead tobacco from the bowl and slowly eased into a standing position. His burly form seemed to tower above the insurgent settlers.

His Swedish lilt carried a mocking tone, "Don't see no *boys'* here, 'cept maybe JP, and he's fast becoming a man. He may have made the leap already, though."

He sent a condescending look down his nose, he added. "The exception might be you *boys,* who likes to call yourselves men."

Tic Underhill bristled at the implied barb.

Some of the other travelers had clustered in small groups on the outskirts to watch and listen.

"When you plan on moving this train again?" he asked.

Cunningham puckered his lips and looked skyward just to infuriate Underhill before answering.

The homesteader let loose with an exaggerated loud sigh at the delay.

Bringing his eyes back down, Micah said, "Not sure."

"Well, ain't that the hell of it!" Tic exploded. "We've been here five days. It's time to move on. Winter's coming and I want my family settled before the snow flies."

Lavanier responded, "Your team rested and wagon repaired? Harnesses fixed?"

"Did that days ago."

James added, "The next stretch will be harder than them redskins swooping down on ya."

A low murmur began circulating through the settlers.

Leaning forward, Underhill asked, "Yeah? And how do you know that?"

"Been that way many times. Hard on a horse. Harder on a wagon."

"You're lying," the greenhorn challenged.

Packy rose abruptly and marched to Underhill and stared at the shorter man. His fist came out of nowhere and landed solid on the settler's jaw. Tic spun with the impact and flew into the arms of his supporters.

Underhill shook his head and scrambled to regain his footing. He was ready to lunge and exchange blows.

Packy stopped him with his words, "I wouldn't if I were you."

Underhill's eyes carried a tad of hesitancy as he gazed at the lean, hard, grizzled face of Woods. His eyes sparkled with anger.

"My friends don't lie. If'n you be in such an all-fire hurry to get going, do it. We'll catch up with ya," he turned his back on the dissidents and walked away. Then, he spun back around and added, "That is if'n y'all ain't dead. If that be the case, we'll make sure ya get a decent burial."

"You're bluffing. Trying to scare us into sticking together," Tic expounded.

"He's not bluffing," Micah said, rising and walking to stand in front of Underhill. "In treks like this, there is safety in numbers."

"Awww! Go to hell!" the settler said. He turned to his followers and added, "Let's go. We're moving out in the morning."

He stopped and let his eyes travel over the spectators and announced, "Anyone else wants to come, we leave at sun-up."

Struggling to stand, Thigpen leaned heavily on JP and

said, "Tic, you're a damn fool!"

The man's eyes darted to Thigpen for a moment before he motioned for his group to leave the small camp.

Elizabeth pushed her way forward and shouted, "Mr. Underhill, wait!"

He turned to stare at her, his face showing disapproval.

"Mr. Underhill, I think you need to heed these men's words," she said, tilting her head and searching his face for some kind sensibility. "If it wasn't for these men finding JP and coming to our aid, we would all be dead a long time ago. They know this land. We don't."

She took a deep breath, looked away from the stubborn man and added, "I just wish they had come sooner. Then, maybe my husband would still be alive."

She glanced around and noticed she had everyone's attention, especially Underhill's.

"We started with fifteen families and wagons. Each one of us had hopes and dreams. You, too. had dreams of a new land, a place to set down new roots and grow freely. The options were limitless.

"Now we are down to ten wagons. If you leave, only seven will remain. As Mr. Cunningham and Mr. Woods pointed out there are safety in numbers, Mr. Underhill."

Tic took a few steps toward the woman, leaning in and angrily replied, "Why don't you just tend to the washing and cooking. Keep your nose outta men's business!"

He looked wickedly at Willis, smiled and added, "Why your man weren't even cold in the ground when ya hooked up with the likes of him. Huh? He keep you warm at night?"

The four huntsmen stepped forward. Each wanted a turn at pummeling the arrogant jackass.

Thigpen shouted, urging JP to move faster toward troublemaker. "I'll get you for that, you yellow-bellied sapsucker!"

Elizabeth gasped and reared back from the venomous words. Recovering quickly, she stood proudly and refused to back down.

"I feel sorry for your missus. I know you intimidate her, just like you tried to do to me. But I won't let you do that. Do you understand, Mr. Underhill?"

"No woman talks to me like that," he growled.

A faint smile slid across Elizabeth's features as she replied, "I just did."

"No woman talks to me like that and gets away with it," he said and raised his hand to strike her. "I know how to make…"

Lavanier leaped across the short space with uncanny speed. His fist landed hard against Underhill's jaw. The bully's head swiveled, teeth flew and blood splattered before he landed in a heap six feet back.

Obsidian eyes shining with anger and disgust, James turned to Underhill's cronies and said, "Get that rotten carcass outta here." He pointed over their shoulders, and added, "At first light, them wagons better be gone."

He dropped his hand and waited to see what the five followers would do. They were too stunned to do anything. They looked from the French-Canadian to the fallen Underhill and back again.

James' voice dropped to a deep, threatening timbre. "Move!" he ordered.

The other three woodsmen stepped closer, boxing in the remaining five followers in a silent threat.

Three of Tic's sons scrambled to pick up their father. Micah and Johan stepped back to let them pass along with the others.

Cunningham and Svenson glanced at each other and smiled. They shrugged the incident off as if it was a normal occurrence. They settled back in a relaxing pose next to the fire.

The spectators slowly disbursed, knowing the entertainment was over. The air was filled with soft murmurs and laughter.

Still supported by his son, Willis touched Elizabeth's arm.

She turned.

"You all right?" he asked softly.

She nodded and replied, "Yes."

Next, she turned to James and added, "Thank you."

"My pleasure, ma'am," he replied.

"When do you think we will move on," she asked of no one in particular.

Packy snorted, "We'll give them sorry jackasses a few days to get lost, first."

Elizabeth grinned, "Then rescue them, again?"

The men chuckled.

"We might have to," Micah said.

"If'n they ain't dead by then," added Packy.

"I understand," Elizabeth replied. She turned to Marah and Colleen and added, "Come along girls. Time for bed."

Her daughters reluctantly rose and followed their mother.

CHAPTER 14

"Damn horse has gone lame on us, Pa," Clay, the oldest Underhill son, announced after examining the front leg of the gelding. "What we gonna do now?"

"Ya gonna shoot it, Pa?" asked the youngest, Verlyn, hopping from one foot to the other in glee.

Ernest, the middle son, scowled at his brother and said, "Ain't no need for that. Just needs some rest."

Verlyn pouted, turning to their father, "That ain't true, is it, Pa? It's no use ta us. So, you're gonna shoot it, right?"

Ernest glanced away and shook his head.

Unlike his two brothers Clay and Verlyn who thought the sun rose and set on their father, Ernest didn't. He had vowed to leave the brood and never look back once they were settled in the new land.

Tic's wife, Maisy, stood apart from the four men, wringing her hands. The deep furrows on her brow looked as if they were dug with a plow, all from years of worry. She knew better than to say something. Tic would slap her silly. How she wished she had stayed with the train, but it was too late now.

Maisy's eyes roamed the terrain. It was rougher now. They were riding into the mountains. Evergreens overshadowed the hardwoods. There was no trail; they were heading northwest blindly. She withheld the deep sigh of despair that wanted to escape. Tic would backhand her if he heard it.

Once a handsome woman, Maisy Underhill was a shadow of her former self. Her eyes were a listless, dull brown and constantly darted about with fear. Her frame had shrunk, her grayish brown hair had thinned and her clothes were unkempt. Her face was pale, accenting the dark circles under her eyes. They resembled bruises.

She wondered how her family had become her enemy. Briefly, she considered taking the lame horse and escaping back to the wagon train. In what direction would she flee, though? The thought baffled her. She sighed deeply, realizing she was trapped and had been for a long time.

Suddenly, she recognized there was only one sure fire method to escape the misery she had dealt with for so many years. She toyed with the idea for a few moments, and then put it aside to study more thoroughly later.

She looked to the cerulean colored sky and wondered if there really was a God. She had known people who prayed, but she had never done so. Maisy didn't even know how to pray, much less what to ask for if she did. She would have to think on that some more, too.

↔

"Naw. we ain't gonna shoot it. Just unhitch it and let it go. The wolves will have a feast."

Ernest disagreed.

"Pa, we's gonna need that gelding," he pleaded as he stepped toward his father. "Ain't no way one team is gonna make it pulling that heavy wagon. If you kill off the horses, you be settin' us afoot."

His eyes narrowed and he boldly added, "'My way of thinking, that ain't real smart."

Bristling at his son's comments, Tic leaned into him and said, "You ain't doing the thinking, boy. I am!"

"Exactly my point," Ernest mocked, knowing it might get him smacked.

"You just shad-up," his father said.

Not backing off, Ernest replied, "One day, Pa. One day, you will get your comeuppance."

Without another word, he turned and grabbed the injured gelding's bridle and slowly walked away.

Glaring at the back of his middle son, Underhill muttered, "Damn fool kid."

The other two wagons had pulled alongside the Underhills and watched the events unfold. It only added to their concern. Not long after separating from the wagon train, the Ropers and Lesters realized they had made a huge mistake by following the irascible and belligerent Tic. They hoped and prayed the rest of the train would be able to find them in the vast wilderness.

Newt Roper called out, "Hey Underhill!"

Tic turned.

"What happened?"

"Horse pulled up lame," he said, squinting against the sun as he walked toward Roper's wagon. "You folks go on ahead, we'll catch up later."

Roper glanced at his wife, who administered a subtle nod and encouraged her husband.

Taking a deep breath, Newt took the plunge, "Uh, the Lesters and us decided this was as good as any place to stop for the night."

Already in a foul mood, Tic's voice echoed through the countryside.

"What? We got three, maybe four, hours of daylight left!" he yelled. He waved his arms wildly and his face turned crimson as he added, "Get on! You're wastin' daylight!"

He punched a fist into the hip of the closest mule for emphasis. The animal jumped and kicked out, hitting the double tree, braying in surprise.

Settling the animals down, Newt reached for the whip

and snapped Underhill across his hat sending it flying. The second lash landed across his shoulders.

Tic whirled, jumped onto hub of the wheel and reached for Newt's shirt.

A fist stopped his charge and send a wad of chew flying through the air. It landed in the thick turf, followed by the short-tempered antagonist. Underhill landed hard, knocking the breath from his lungs.

Roper stood with the whip recoiled and ready to strike again. His eyes locked with the wild ones of Underhill.

"You do not touch my stock," he warned. "From now on, we no longer will be associated with you or your family."

Before Underhill could regain his breath, Roper slapped the reins against the rumps of his team and moved out, followed by the Lester family.

Tic regained his feet and spun like a deranged animal. Unaccustomed to the treatment he received from Roper, he was furious. His eyes darted about, looking for a target. He spotted his wife and middle son.

"Maisy! Get your behind back to the wagon. We're moving out!" Tic shouted. "And bring that boy along with ya."

An involuntary shudder rippled through Maisy. Filled with fear, she looked to Ernest for help, but knew her son was no match for his ill-tempered father. When her husband was angry, he was unpredictable.

Silence filled the landscape.

She turned away from her son and slowly trudged toward their wagon.

"Ma, wait!" Ernest called.

Maisy stopped, closed her eyes and waited.

"Ma, you don't have to go." Ernest said, coming alongside her. "I'm not."

She gasped and couldn't believe her ears.

Her son nodded toward the draw where the Lesters and Ropers were and added. "I think they will take us in until someone from the train finds us."

Looking at her son, "You sure?"

He grinned and replied, "No, but I'm hopeful. They're good people, Ma."

Maisy took a deep breath and exhaled slowly. She was fraught indecision.

"But your father…"

Her son's face grew hard. His eyes flashed with anger and he said, "I'm done. I don't give a rat's ass what happens to him."

Maisy gasped.

His face softened when he saw the distress in his mother's face.

"You don't have to take it anymore either, Ma. You and me could start a new life and be happy for once."

His mother frowned, "But your father has all our money and our things."

"I know. But I'm able bodied and can work," Ernest said, glancing at the two families already setting up camp in the draw. "It'll take some doing, but I think we can make it."

A thin, blue-veined hand patted his arm as a small smile brightened his mother's face. She sighed and said, "All right then. We'll try."

Sliding her arm into the crook of his elbow, the two began the walk toward the settlers, leading the limping horse behind them.

Climbing into the wagon seat with Clay and Verlyn, Underhill waited on his wife and lazy son. When they didn't arrive fast enough to suit him, he tossed a look around the canvas bonnet. His eyes went wide with shock and then narrowed in anger.

"That damn woman," he muttered, punching Clay in the arm,

"Ouch! Pa, that hurt," Clay said, rubbing his upper limb.

Tic ordered sharply, "Go get your mother and brother."

Scrambling over Verlyn's legs, Clay hopped down and trotted behind the wagon. When he was close enough for them to hear him, he said, "Pa says for you to come to the wagon. We're leaving."

Maisy hesitated.

Ernest's firm grip on her hand kept her moving forward.

"Hey? Didn't y'all hear me? Pa says..."

"You go right ahead with him," Ernest said sternly and steered his mother down the slope. "Me and Ma is staying here."

Clay was dumbfounded by his brother's defiant tone. He was speechless for a moment but finally said, "But Pa..."

Dropping his mother's hand, the middle son reeled on his brother. With teeth gritted he proclaimed, his baritone carrying a firm message, "We ain't coming. We ain't puttin' up with his ways no more."

He spat in the dirt and waved his arm at his brother saying, "Now, you scat! Go back to that old man. We ain't!"

Earnest glared at his brother for a few more seconds. Then, he reached for his mother's hand, turned and walked away.

Clay stood there dumbstruck. He couldn't believe his ears. Finally finding his voice, he shouted, "You and Ma is gonna pay for that! You hear me, Ernest? You is gonna pay!"

Maisy hesitated and said, "Ernest, I don't know?"

He kept a firm hold of her hand and said, "No, Ma. Keep walking. We're done, remember?"

Drawing a shaky breath, she nodded and kept moving.

The low wind had carried part of the exchange to the camp. Settlers stopped to watch and listen.

The pair strode into the encampment. Shock filled the faces of the Roper and Lester families. The silence was unnerving. Finally, Ernest cleared his throat in order to speak.

"No need, son," Newt Roper began, "You are welcome to stay with us. We don't blame you for leaving."

"Thank you, sir," he replied and smiled for the first time in weeks.

Overcome with emotion and relief, Maisy sank to her knees. Tears ran like a fast-moving stream down her cheeks, leaving white tracks. Her voice cracked. All she could do was whisper, "Thank you."

Liza Roper and Naomie Lester glanced at each other without saying a word. They stepped quickly to Mrs. Underhill's sides, helped her to her feet and led her to their wagons.

↔

Reluctant to climb into the wagon, knowing his father would use him as a punching bag when he relayed the news, Clay walked up to the wagon and urged his father to move the team.

"Where's your mother and brother?" he asked.

Taking a deep breath, Clay told him: "They's not comin', Pa."

Yanking on the reins, Tic yelled, "What? Don't you dare lie to me, boy?"

Vigorously shaking his head, Clay couldn't look up at his father. He stared at the ground and said, "No, Pa. It's the truth."

Stunned at the news the youngest boy's jaw dropped open. Verlyn looked at his father tearfully and asked, "Ma ain't coming? Who's gonna fix our food?"

Tic peered around the bonnet, his eyes fixated on the draw where the two families had set up camp, He spat a stream of brown juice, cementing his next words, "Aw, let 'em rot in hell. We don't need 'em. They was never no good no how!"

He slapped the reins, and the three horses began pulling the heavy wagon forward. His boys didn't say a word.

CHAPTER 15

"I swear! I think Curtright jinxed this train," Packy bellowed, wiping the sweat from his brow and resettling his hat after helping to put a wheel back on one of the wagons. "I ain't never seen folks have so much bad luck in all my born days. They was s'posed to fix this stuff. That's why we laid up a week!" He shook his head in frustration.

Chuckling, Johan added, "That's cause you ain't used ta working, Packy boy."

Throwing the big Swede a dirty look, Packy replied, "The hell ya say! I pull my fair share!"

"Most times." said Micah with a big grin.

James leaned in and, with a straight face, added, "Maybe it's them forest fairies causing all the trouble."

Packy's head swung, staring in wonder at the French-Canadian. "What forest fairies?" he asked.

"Mischief makers."

"Huh?"

"Leprechauns," chimed in Micah, trying to hold back

the laughter.

Packy frowned. When he saw the amusement on his comrades' faces, he sputtered and said, "Aw, get along with y'all!"

He mounted his mule and proclaimed, "We need to get a move on. Which way, James?"

James pointed west and said, "Got another few days' for we get to the Platte River, if I recall right. Once we cross, we head a little south on other side of the Platte. Then, we need to go through the South Pass and on to Fort Hall."

"Well, that sounds simple enough, baring anymore problems," Packy remarked. He booted his mule to the front of the small train to act as lookout.

"Ya, be nice to have an easy passage for once," Johan suggested.

James called out one last time before Packy was beyond hearing distance. "Watch out fer them leprechauns, pard! Never know when they may pounce on ya!"

The lanky woodsman threw a dirty look over his shoulder but didn't let the goading bother him.

The three enjoyed the laughter at Packy's expense. They knew they might not get the opportunity again, given the sobering journey that lay ahead. They mounted and fanned out around the train pushing them into motion.

↔

Everyone was eager to rest around the campfire at the end of the day. Driving the teams and wagons for twelve miles was grueling. Not much conversation was generated because, tired as they all were, they knew the journey would restart early on the morrow.

Restless, JP blurted out, "Mr. Cunningham, do you think we'll find those other three wagons?"

Packy snorted. "More'n likely find 'em dead."

Elizabeth gasped and scolded, "Mr. Woods! That's an awful thing to say!"

Packy turned pink.

Micah spoke, "He's not far from the truth, Mrs. Livingston."

"It might be, but still it's not kind," she insisted as she refilled their cups with coffee.

Sipping his, Lavanier threw out his two-cents worth. "Even after all the months of traveling, you folks are still a bunch a shavetails," he said.

Twelve-year old Marah piped up, "What's that?"

All eyes converged on the child, who was surprised to be the center of attention suddenly. Her shoulders rose and her palms spread wide. "What?" she asked with questioning eyes.

James clarified, "Means a greenhorn."

"Or just plain ol' green," tossed in Packy.

"Green like what?" she pursued.

Willis Thigpen stepped in to explain.

"We're farm families," he said, raising an arm into the air and sweeping it across the campfire to include the rest of the travelers. "That's been our lives until we decided to do this. We know nothin' about any of this. It requires a different mindset than any of us has ever experienced. So, folks refer to us as green, greenhorns or shavetails."

Marah's eyes brightened and she said, 'Ah!'

Micah agreed and complimented the speaker, "Nicely said, Mr. Thigpen."

Willis smiled back, "Thank you, Mr. Cunningham.

"Girls? Time for bed," Mrs. Livingston declared

"Aww, Ma!"

"Scoot! We'll be up while the stars are still high in the sky," Elizabeth said, ushering the girls into the wagon.

"Ya," Svenson said, lightly banging his clay pipe against a piece of wood. "That's for sure."

Turning to the lad, Micah said, "JP, I want you to bring fresh stock to each one of the wagons first thing in the morning."

"Yes sir."

Cunningham let a faint smile escape under the unruly growth of beard at the politeness of the boy. "You get some sleep, too," he added.

"Yes sir." JP said and sauntered off to his wagon.

When the lad was out of earshot, Micah remarked, "You're raising a fine boy, Thigpen."

"Thank you," Willis said, watching his son settle down for the night. "With your help he'll make a great man one day. You keep teaching him what you know. He learns quick."

"Ya, he do remember," Johan said, removing his pipe from his mouth and pointing the stem at the wagon, "He remember real good."

The call to move out echoed down the line while the stars were still in full glory. Trace chains jingled, wheels creaked and wagons shuddered as the four-ups and two-ups leaned into their harnesses and heaved forward. The lumbering wagons began to roll.

Adults and children walked alongside keeping pace but most were half asleep.

JP and others kept the remuda moving.

Woods and Cunningham rode off ahead to scout the area. Secretly, they wondered if they would run upon the three wagons that went off by themselves. More importantly, what would they find if they did?

"Well, Pa, now what?" Clay remarked looking at the disabled wagon.

Tic Underhill grunted disgustedly. He scooted from under the bed after peering at the broken axel, dusted himself off and squinted at his boys.

"Unhitch them horses, we'll ride," he said.

Underhill wasn't about to let his sons know he was almost done. His pride wouldn't let him. They were lost, and he knew it, but he had a reputation as their fearless leader to maintain.

Verlyn looked in the wagon, "What about our stuff, Pa?"

Tic took a deep breath and examined the terrain around them. It looked more than rough.

"We'll pack what we need and ride," he ordered.

"But why? What's gonna happen to all our things?" Verlyn insisted.

Underhill's anger rose like a wildfire. He pounced on the boy. Verlyn's arms quickly covered his head and face to ward off any blows.

Eyes flashing with anger, Tic yelled, "Ain't you heard me, boy? I said we's gonna pack what we need and ride. Now, you get in there and start tossing out stuff we need."

Peeking through his arms, Verlyn's lower lip began to quiver and tears rolled down his dirty cheeks. He disregarded his father's directive and said, "I want Ma."

Whirling, Underhill backhanded the lad and sent him flying.

"Quit ya sniveling. Your ma is dead. She ain't coming back. Now, get in that wagon and toss out what we need!" he ordered, glaring at his youngest for a few moments before spinning on his toes and walking away.

"She ain't neither!" cried Verlyn. "She and Ernest is with the Ropers!"

Rounding and taking a couple steps toward his son, the patriarch scolded, "If'n ya know what's good for ya, you'll get in that wagon!"

Tear-filled eyes looked to brother Clay for help.

His older brother quickly looked away.

Verlyn knew help was not coming. Clay was afraid of their father, too. His hand swiped at his runny nose. He wiped the snot on his britches, sniffled and climbed into the wagon.

Topping a ridge, Woods and Cunningham reined in their mounts and gazed at the terrain before them. It reminded them of a wrinkled quilt after someone had a restless night. The landscape was marked by a few jagged peaks, soft ridges and pockets of granite. It was if they had been dumped from a bucket by some unseen force.

The sun was behind them warming their backs.

Shifting in his saddle, Packy remarked, "Nice country."

"Ain't it though," Micah said with a nod of agreement.

The wind shifted and Packy's nose wiggled.

"Say, do I smell smoke?" he said.

Lifting his chin, Micah breathed deep. "Yep."

"Thought so."

"Northwest."

"Little bit off trail, but not by much." Packy observed.

"Could be our lost wagons.

"Or not."

"True," finished Micah.

Neither said a word about what they expected to find if they decided to follow their noses.

Curiosity won out. Heels softly nudged ribs and the two headed toward the smoke trail.

Svenson and Lavanier kept the wagons moving at what felt like a snail's pace. They both knew the settlers had packed way too much in their schooners. It was making it difficult on the teams to keep a good steady pace.

JP and others had the remuda under control. They were riding drag behind the homesteaders.

Bringing up the rear, Willis instructed Elizabeth to fan out from the line of wagons so they wouldn't have to eat so much dust. Thigpen was gaining his strength back day by day. He still tired easily, though.

Marah ran alongside the wagon to where her mother was seated. "Mama? she called out.

Elizabeth looked down.

"Can we ride for a while? We're tired."

Pulling on the reins, Elizabeth halted the team, looked at her girls and said, "Climb in. If you're hungry, you know where the jerky is."

Climbing over her mother, Marah threw a smile at Thigpen, then kissed her mama on the cheek. Before she climbed into the back, she added, "Thanks, Mama."

Colleen scrambled in next and thanked her mother, too.

"You're welcome," she said, glancing at Willis. She let a smile bloom across her features before slapping the rumps of the team with the reins.

Elizabeth looked over her shoulder at her daughters and offered, "There's a canteen back there, too, if you're thirsty."

Mumbling around a mouthful of hard jerky, Marah

answered, "Thanks, Mama."

Silence reigned, except for the trace chains jingling and the bumps and thumps of the wheels as they pounded against uneven ground, hidden by the grassy terrain.

Abruptly, Elizabeth's soft voice blurted out, "What do you think it will be like?"

Thigpen had been deep within his own thoughts. He'd grown to enjoy Elizabeth's company and was toying with the idea of asking her to marry him when they reached Fort Hall. He jerked to attention when he heard her voice.

"Huh? Did you say something?" he asked.

"Yes," she replied, her twinkling eyes flashing him a quick look. She knew she had caught him deep in thought. "I asked, what do you think it will be like?"

"Be like?" he scratched his head trying to figure out where she was going with her question.

"Oregon," she said simply.

"Oh," he said, taking a few moments to gather his thoughts before giving her a steady gaze. "Honestly? I don't know."

She nodded but wanted more of an answer.

"It could be paradise, or it could be hell. We won't know until we get there," Willis said. Catching a glimpse of Johan and James in the distance, he pointed and added, "I'll bet those two fellers know what we can expect there."

"All right, we can ask them at supper tonight."

"I'd be interested to know what they have to say," Willis added.

"Me too."

He grinned at her answer.

Elizabeth returned the smile.

Following the smoke trail, the two huntsmen topped a ridge and stared down the hill to see two wagons had set up an encampment.

"Reckon we found our lost wagons," volunteered Packy.

"Maybe. Kinda hard to recognize anyone from this distance."

"Who else could it be?" Packy asked.

"Let's find out."

Spotting the two riders approaching, someone in the small group yelled, "Visitors!"

Hearing the call, men rushed to grab their weapons, shooing the women and children inside the wagons or behind them.

Relief spread across Newt Roper's face when he recognized who was riding into their camp.

"Well, I'll be," he said, stepping forward to greet old friends, "You boys sure are a sight for sore eyes." He turned quickly to his wife and said, "Liza, get these boys some coffee and grub."

Micah stepped out of the saddle and advanced to take Roper's hand.

Roper was so full of enthusiasm; he pumped the trapper's arm like he was going to drain the well. "How'd you boys find us? We's been praying mighty hard ya would."

"Campfire smoke," was the simple reply.

"That's mighty good tracking if ya ask me," replied Royce Lester.

"Aww, shucks!" said Packy, "T'weren't nuthin'. We do it all the time."

"Well, we sure is glad you showed up," Lester admitted.

The four men walked closer to the camp. Liza handed Micah and Packy their plates and coffee. Without hesitation, she urged them to sit and eat.

"Underhill was leading us on a wild goose chase. Running our horses to ground. There's no telling what else he might have pulled, if'n we hadn't left him when we did," volunteered Royce.

Cunningham and Woods listened intently and shared a knowing glance.

Talking around a mouthful of food, Micah squinted and directed the question to Roper, "Where is he now?"

"God only knows," Lester said.

Nodding, he shoveled more food.

"His missus and one his boys joined us," Newt informed.

Packy's head bounced up and he said, "Ya don't say?"

Liza refilled their cups.

Maisy Underhill timidly approached. When she spoke, her voice was a thin whisper. "Do you think you could find my boys?" she asked.

Micah rose towering over the small, bent-framed woman. Studying her as he handed the plate back to Mrs. Roper. He drained his coffee cup before asking, "What about your husband, Mrs. Underhill?"

Her son, Ernest, pushed through the small crowd gathered and blurted out, "He can rot in hell."

Mrs. Underhill gasped, spun and scolded her son, "Ernest, hold your tongue!"

Packy's eyes darted, constantly watching and listening to the exchange. He never stopped shoveling food into his mouth, though.

Ernest gazed at his mother for a few moments, then back to Cunningham, "Just find my brothers and bring them back here," he asked. "Please? It would make my ma happy."

Micah turned, "Packy? You 'bout done filling your belly? Seems we got some boys to find."

Uncorking his long limbs and shoveling forkfuls into to his mouth, Packy stood and nodded. He swallowed hastily and slurped the last of his coffee. When he handed his plate and cup to Mrs. Roper, he said, "Mighty fine, ma'am. Mighty fine!"

As he followed Micah back to their horses, Packy let a huge belch escape as he mounted. Micah cut him a cockeyed look, addressed Maisy as he climbed back into the leather.

"We'll bring your boys back, Mrs. Underhill," he said. He and Packy trotted back to the ridgetop.

Overcome with emotion Maisy's eyes glistened with grateful tears. Ernest wrapped an arm about his mother's shoulders to comfort her.

Maisy slid an arm around her son's waist and had a good feeling as she watched the riders crest the ridge and disappear.

CHAPTER 16

"JP, we'll be stopping for a break soon," James said, riding up next to the lad. "Need you to get fresh teams for these wagons."

"Yes, sir."

"Grab some food and water for yourself, too. We'll be on the move soon after."

"Where's Packy and Mr. Cunningham?" JP asked.

"Scouting."

"Reckon they'll find them other wagons?"

"Might. Might not." James replied.

JP let a huge sigh escape and said, "I hope so. I liked Ernest and Verlyn. Clay not so much."

Chuckling, James said, "As you grow older, you'll find many you won't like so much."

"I guess," JP said, mystified.

"Start rounding up them teams."

"Yes, sir."

Watching the kid ride off and begin signaling the others to sort fresh teams for the wagons, James allowed a smile to lift the corners of his mouth. Reining around, James headed for Johan. He already was sounding the call for a break.

Halting next to the Thigpen wagon, Svenson watched Willis gingerly climb down from the seat box. When his feet touched the ground the Swede said, "It won't be long now. You'll be dancin' a jig 'round da fire."

Looking up and squinting against the sun, Willis grinned. "One day," he said as he limped forward to unhitch the team and wait on fresh ones.

Johan dismounted and helped from the other side. Slipping the bridle off and unbuckling the collar. Out of the blue, Svenson asked, "How's you and Mrs. Livingston getting along?"

Thigpen's hands stilled. He looked across at the big Swede and then let his eyes flicker toward Elizabeth. She bustled about making coffee and fixing a quick meal.

"We are working well together," he said and returned his attention to the harness.

"Gonna find me a good woman one day," remarked Johan. "Don't know where out here, but I will."

Willis just nodded. He was going to try and hang on to the one he'd found if she would let him.

"Willis? Johan? Come get something to eat," called

Elizabeth. Shielding her eyes from the sun's glare, "Where's JP and James?"

"They be coming in shortly, ma'am."

"Good," she said.

Scooting out from under the disabled wagon, Packy finally drew his frame to its full lanky height. Whipping off his battered felt hat, grungy fingers scratched his scalp and wiped the sweat drizzling down the side of his face. He resettled the felt on his head, placed his hands on his hips and asked, "How in the hell did Underhill let this happen?"

Micah had wandered away, shutting out Packy's ramblings. That long drink of water was a master at talking and never really said much worth hearing. Micah had learned to ignore his ramblings. Cunningham was more interested in the trail he had found. He kneeled to review the tracks.

"Hey! Did ya hear me?" Packy asked.

"We got more interesting things going on here than a broken-down wagon," Micah said, pointing to the hoof prints. "Tracks head down there."

"Three horses, and they are carrying a considerable load."

"Yup. Only a day old, too," Packy said.

In unison, both men mounted and began following the

trail.

Checking on the remuda, JP was satisfied all was quiet. He enjoyed being head wrangler for the wagon train, and hoped he was making his father proud.

Glancing at the peaceful scene of folks gathering around campfires, triggered a wave of happiness. It had been a long hard road so far, and there was no telling what lay ahead. It didn't matter. JP loved the adventure of it all, especially when the heroic mountain men rescued him and joined the train. Without them, the settlers wouldn't be alive.

He dismounted at the Thigpen wagon and removed the tack from his horse. He immediately grabbed a plate and sat cross-legged by the fire. His eyes darted around while shoveling in potatoes and meat. He took a minute to ask, "I don't see Mr. Cunningham and Packy. Are they not back yet?"

"Nope," answered Lavanier.

"Why not? Thought they would have been back by now?" the young boy asked.

Shrugging, Svenson said wryly, "Might be lost."

Chuckles filled the air.

JP rejected the idea. "Lost? Surely not them?" he said.

Willis grinned, recognizing his son's growing

admiration for the woodsmen. "No, never lost. Maybe they have found something that's keeping them from returning," he suggested.

"Gosh, I hope they're not hurt someplace." JP said.

"Those two? Never!" added James.

While they were all together, Elizabeth took advantage of the moment to ask the question that had been burning in her mind all day. "Mr. Lavanier, you've been farther west, haven't you?"

James glanced up from his plate when he heard his name. The woman's eyes were briming with curiosity. He responded quickly, "Yessum."

She tilted her head and asked, "What's it like?"

"Temperate in the valleys, snow on the peaks. Heavily forested. Good water and land in the valleys. Depends on where you settle and what you want to do with the land you choose as your own. Don't think you will have many neighbors or a town as of yet. Land is still too young."

"I see," Elizabeth said.

James noted disappointment in her tone and added, "I could be wrong. Haven't been there for some time. But I think you will like it there."

"Thank you. I hope I will. It will be nice to settle somewhere.""

150

A low wind blew a tantalizing scent across their noses. Both trappers halted their mounts, sat easy and listened.

Wolves cried their plaintive howl to the starlit sky. Others answered. Owls hooted. Hawks beat their wings through the still air, looking for prey.

The dampness of the night had arrived. No moon shined from above, just millions of stars shinning their weak light upon the land. Shapes of trees and granite faces were outlined in silhouette against a dark backdrop that was speckled with pinpricks of light.

Rolling a well-used piece of tobacco around with his tongue, Packy spit a stream of juice and said, "I reckon we's found Underhill."

"Maybe. Won't know 'til we get there," Micah reasoned, nudging his tired horse into a walk. The dingy mule followed.

The scent of wood smoke grew stronger. Soon three individuals hunched over a fire came into view.

"Hi-lo, in the camp," Cunningham called out.

Three bodies, startled, jumped to attention. They all stared into the darkness, hoping to find a friendly face.

Packy grinned at their response. Guiding his mule alongside Micah's roan, the woodsmen entered the circle of firelight.

Recognizing the two mountain men, Tic Underhill growled, "What do the likes of you want?"

A brow inched up at the surly response, but Micah's face remained deadpanned. "Share your fire?" was his simple reply."

"We ain't got enough for two more," came the gruff reply.

"No need. We got our own grub."

Instead of answering, Tic shrugged and turned his back on the two visitors.

Packy spit out the wad of old tobacco and dismounted. He striped the mule of its gear and dropped it closer to the fire. Micah did the same with his gear. Three sets of eyes followed every move the trappers made.

Pulling some jerky from a leather pouch, Cunningham leaned back against his saddle and bit off a hunk of dried meat and began softening it up in his mouth.

Beady eyes glared at him. "What you boys doing here?" Underhill asked.

"Looking for you," Cunningham replied.

Clay and Verlyn stared at the visitors.

"You threw us off the train," Underhill said.

"True."

"Saw your busted wagon back yonder," added Packy.

Underhill's eyes darted to the lanky woodsman, for whom he held no respect.

"So?" Tic said smartly.

"Shame. Nice wagon."

The air seemed to bristle with tension. Underhill's unfriendly attitude seemed to fan out and envelope everyone.

"What do you want?" he asked.

Gesturing toward the lads, Micah said, "Their ma wants them back."

"Like hell!" Underhill snarled.

Micah ignored the troublemaker, looked directly at the boys and said, "You want to go back? We'll take ya."

A myriad of emotions swept through the lads' eyes. Excitement. Relief. Confusion. Finally, disappointment settled in as they resigned themselves to stay with their father.

Micah said what the boys were afraid to admit, "You don't have to stay with him."

Underhill bounced from the ground and advanced on Cunningham with balled fists.

"Now, you see here!" he shouted. "You ain't got no right ta talk ta my boys, that-a-way."

The muscles in Packy's legs tensed. He was ready to spring into action.

Not fazed one lick, Micah calmly gazed at Underhill and stated, "Just saying what I'm sure the boys are feeling."

"And how would you know what my boys are feeling?" Tic asked sarcastically.

Micah snickered and pointed. "Look at them. It's written all over their faces," he said.

Clay and Verlyn kept their eyes downcast, shoulders hunched forward as if to ward off any coming blows. They had no desire to incite their father's wrath.

Tic spun. Took a few steps, "Clay? Verlyn?"

Clay looked up, then flicked his eyes away and said, "What Pa?"

Tic's eyes narrowed.

Verlyn kept his eyes on the ground.

Packy had heard enough and decided to inject his two-cents worth. He rose and refilled his coffee first. He gestured with the cup and said, "Knew a man once upon a time. You remind me of him, Underhill."

A faint smile spread under Micah's bearded face. Packy was about to unleash some of his craziness. He tore off another hunk of jerky and chewed slowly. He had no idea what his friend would spin this time.

Tic whirled to listen.

"Why that man was like a bull gone plumb crazy. He picked fights with anyone who didn't agree with him. He enjoyed bustin' heads. He was kinda like a bull kept in a small pen with barely enough room ta turn about. When that

154

bull was let go he rammed anything and everyone who stood in his way."

Packy pointed the cup at the boys' father, "Kinda like you."

Verlyn had been listening closely to Packy's story and piped up, "What happened to the bull?"

All eyes shifted to the youngster.

"Well, I'll tell ya. That bull died, right unpleasantly too.."

"Why?" the boy asked.

"It had something eating away at its innards so bad it killed him," Packy said.

"And the man?"

"Same thing. Something was eating away at him so fierce, it killed him, too."

Packy zeroed in on Underhill and flatly said, "Like what will happen to you."

Tic's swallowed hard and his eyes flashed with anger. "You lie!" he barked.

The long drip of water shrugged, tossed the remains of coffee and settled down next to his comrade. The only thing he said was, "Suit yourself."

Packy hit the nail on the head, this time.

Clearing his throat, Micah added there was no need for

a hasty decision.

"Let's all get some sleep. Let the boys think on it until morning," he said.

Packy and Micah set up a night camp nearby so the boys and their overbearing father could have some privacy.

CHAPTER  17

Liza Roper dropped a blanket across Mrs. Underhill's shoulders, gently smoothed the material and said, "Maisy, why don't you go get some rest?"

Shaking her head, Maisy said, "No. No, I'll wait." Then, she returned her eyes to the ridge from where she prayed her sons would return.

Mrs. Roper sighed and tried to comfort the thin and frail woman. "Those men know this wilderness. I'm sure they have already found Clay and Verlyn," she said.

"I hope so."

Liza took Maisy's hand and pleaded, "Let's get some rest. Tomorrow will be brighter."

Liza smiled into a time-worn face that appeared much older than its years. "In fact, I know it will be," she added.

Gently, she guided the tattered woman back to camp.

Once again the call went down the line well before

there was a slim line of color gracing the eastern horizon. It was time to get the train moving. The early morning stillness felt almost deafening. Voices chattered to teams of horses and mules as they hitched them to the wagons. Cows bellowed in protest, unhappy to be leaving lush grazing grounds.

The endless trail stretched for miles before them. Weary travelers remained anxious to reach the end of the long journey and begin a new life in their new homes.

Quiet voices conversed as they plodded alongside the wagons. They marched silently, focusing on one step at a time, one minute at a time.

Lavanier and Svenson scouted ahead. They planned to keep the train headed in a northwesterly direction toward the Platte River. From there, they would cross and head on to Fort Hall. They still had lots of wide-open prairies in front of them.

Reining up, the men sat still. Their mounts shuffled, making leather creak. The horses were anxious to be on the move.

Four ears listened to the silence. A low wind ruffled the tall grasses, creating a raspy sound. Prairie chickens sounded their early morning call. A hawk swooped near to the ground, screeching his disdain at the intruders and flew away.

Hitching around in his saddle, Johan studied the coming sun. "Looks to be a good day to make some miles."

Glancing over his shoulder, James saw the redness of the rising sun. "Storms will be here in the next three days."

"Huh? Where do ya see that?" Johan asked.

Grinning, James answered, "For starters, it's in the Holy Book and has been passed down with various versions ever since. It's said: 'Red sky at morn, be forewarned; red sky at night, be your delight.'"

"Harumph! Never heard it before," the Swede said. Blue eyes pierced dark ones, "So, what's gonna happen?"

James nodded east, "Getting redder, so a big storm of some kind will probably hit us soon."

Leaning on his saddle horn, Johan challenged the prediction. "Ya be willing ta wager on it?" he asked.

Shaking his head, "Naw, we'll just wait and see what tomorrow brings."

"Ya chicken?"

James chuckled and replied, "Let's ride out a little farther and see what it looks like for the wagons."

As they nudged their horses forward. Johan added, "Ya, you be chicken."

After saddling his roan and checking the cinch, Micah gazed at the sky. A cerulean blue was plastered from horizon to horizon. A few wispy clouds rode the currents as did a lone eagle and several buzzards.

Mare's tails! Gonna be a change in the weather in three days.

Blue eyes came to rest on the Underhill men who sat around the morning campfire. The boys were subdued. Tic was silent. Oddly, Packy was quiet, too.

Woods felt eyes on him and looked up to find Cunningham staring at him. Their eyes locked for a few moments.

Heaving air, Micah shook his head and walked toward the trio, mentally bracing himself for what might come.

"Well, you lads make up your minds, yet?" he asked.

His words caught Clay and Verlyn by surprise. Heads popped up, looked at the massive woodsman and then at each other. Their eyes reverted to the ground, though, and neither spoke a word.

Tic's head swung up. Beady eyes squinted at Micah as he replied, "They're staying with me."

Micah's posture challenged Underhill. "You sure 'bout that? You ask them?"

Rising slowly, Tic was ready to make a stand. His belligerent demeanor did not go unnoticed by Cunningham.

"No need. Them boys do as I say," the father said.

"I see that."

His gazed dropped to Verlyn and Clay. Turmoil was written all over their faces. So, Micah pressed on, refusing to be bullied.

"What about it? You staying or going back to your ma with me and Packy?"

The kids shifted uncomfortably.

The father leaned forward and glared at his sons. "Go on and tell him. Tell him, you're staying with me," he ordered.

The two glanced at each other. Then, they stood to face their father. Clay looked toward the big Scotch-Irishman as if to gain strength from him before he spoke. Micah's nod encouraged him.

Taking a deep breath, Clay's voice squeaked at first. He cleared his throat, and proclaimed, "We're going with them."

Tic's big mitt lashed out and cuffed Clay hard upside his head. The blow spun Clay around. He hit the ground violently and laid still.

"That's enough, Pa!" Verlyn screamed, running to his brother's side. "We're tired of you beating us for no reason! We're going with them. We're going back to Ma!"

Tears streamed down the young boy's face as he wrapped up all he had to say in one epitaph, "And we're not coming back!"

Sobbing, he bent over his unconscious brother,

seemingly cleansing the hurt and anguish of the past years from his soul. Moccasins crept silently until Micah stood next to Underhill. He tapped the man's shoulder.

Tic whirled, unleashing his rage. "They're my kids, I can do what I want," he roared.

Cunningham's calm exterior contradicted the fury swirling within. He waited.

"What?" Underhill demanded.

"Just this…" the frontiersman said.

As quick as a lightning bolt hitting a lone pine, Micah's fist connected with an uppercut to Underhill's jaw. It lifted him airborne and sent him flying ten feet backward. His head smacked a log near the fire so hard it bounced twice as his body slid into a heap. Tic didn't move.

Flexing his sore knuckles, Micah and watched Packy administer aid to Clay. The kid was coming around after the blow he took from his brutal father.

Verlyn's hand swiped at the tears running down his cheeks, smearing the dirt and giving his features a dappled effect.

Cunningham walked to where Underhill rested. He looked for movement in the man's chest but saw none. Muttering under his breath, he said, "Ye t'were a daft bloke, fer sure, Tic Underhill. You'll not be hurting another soul ever again."

Quickly, he turned and walked back to Packy and

inquired about the boys. "How's the lad?" he asked.

"He'll have a throbbing in his head like a buff stampede, but he'll live," Packy said with a grin.

"Pa?" asked Verlyn.

"Still out cold," Micah lied.

Licking dry lips, the kid nodded and said, "Now, we can safely go to Ma?"

"If your brother is able to ride."

Sitting up holding his head, Clay whispered, "I will be if I can get some water."

The youngest scrambled to retrieve a canteen and handed it to his brother. Nodding his thanks, Clay took a swig and lowered his head back into his arms.

Thumbing over his shoulder, Micah said to Verlyn, "C'mon kid. Let's go saddle those horses." Packy stayed to make sure Clay was fully recovered.

Hanging back from the two boys riding ahead, Packy whispered a question that had been burning in his mind since they left the camp. "Is Underhill dead?"

A slight nod provided the answer.

"Figured so the way his head bounced off that log was a good sign," he said.

"Yup." Micah said.

"I reckon it'll be a blessing to those folks."

"Yup." Micah added. "Now, she's got three strapping boys. She'll be all right."

"You gonna tell them?"

"Not if I don't have to. Best they think he went off into the wilderness on his own."

"Yup."

Approaching the disabled wagon, Cunningham asked, "You boys need anything from here? Get it now."

The two looked at each other, then at the trappers. "We don't know," Clay said. "Ma is the one who would know what we need."

Packy looked at his partner and suggested, "Think we could make a new axel? Get this wagon back on the trail again?"

Micah frowned as he mulled the idea over in his mind. "Possible. Once we get the rest of the train here. "We'll need some manpower to do that."

"Roper and Lester could cut the log. When the rest came, all of us together could do it," Packy offered up.

"That's what it would take," Micah replied. Then he looked at the boys and added, "Let's get you to your mother first."

"Maisy! Maisy, look!" Ally Lester shouted and pointing off in the distance.

The settlers stopped what they were doing and surrounded the surprised woman. All eyes focused on the four riders who approached.

Immediately, the lads hopped off their horses. They ran and wrapped their arms around their mother. Ernest joined the joyful reunion.

"As promised, Mrs. Underhill, here are your sons," Micah said.

Tears ran in rivets down Maisy's face. When she had time to address the woodsmen, she said, "You truly are a man of your word, Mr. Cunningham. And you, too, Mr. Woods. Thank you. Thank you both."

"Roper? Lester? Get ready to roll," Micah ordered. "Got a broken axel on the Underhill wagon, which ain't far from here. Need it fixed so Mrs. Underhill and her sons can travel with the rest of us."

Maisy ran to Micah, pulled on his sleeve and asked, "My husband?"

Micah remained silent.

Packy offered, "Last we seen of him, ma'am, he was unconscious."

A frown puckered Maisy's face. Her brow furrowed as

she asked, "What happened?"

"Well, your husband knocked Clay there plumb stupid," Packy explained.

Maisy whirled to stare at her son.

"He did, Ma," Clay attested.

"Micah didn't take kindly to what he did to the boy. So, he and Micah had a… ah… kind of a one-sided dustup. We loaded up the boys and left him there."

Micah intervened, "He won't be bothering you or your sons anymore, ma'am."

Looking at the dark-haired woodsman, Maisy searched for the truth. Finally, she said, "He's dead, ain't he?"

"Yessum," Packy admitted.

She gasped, uncertain of what that meant for her and her family's future.

"You have three good boys, Mrs. Underhill," Micah interjected.

She gave a slight bob of her head, still trying to take hold of the fact she was free of her brutal husband.

"You will be just fine," Packy said, trying to reassure her.

Maisy turned to her sons and pulled them close.

Averting his eyes, Micah focused on the homesteaders, "Roper, get your flock moving. The lads can show you where their wagon is. Me and Packy'll go back to the main train. We'll all meet back there."

As the two huntsmen rode over the ridge and disappeared, Roper barked, "You heard the man. Get a move on. We's got a wagon to fix," Roper shouted.

CHAPTER 18

"Think you can hack that log into an axel?" Willis Thigpen asked Newt Roper.

"It'll take some whittlin', but I've done it before," he replied, eyeballing the broken axel next to the new wood. "Main thing is to get it right so the hubs slide on nice and comfy to their new home."

Thigpen grinned.

"Royce here is gonna help. He's made his own before. too."

"Holler, if ya need anything," Willis offered, before limping away.

Roper and Lester began the slow process of carving the new axel.

Watching Newt and Royce patiently carve the green wood into a new axel, Elizabeth remarked, "Byron, never had to do that, but he knew wagons. He kept ours in good shape."

Her eyes roamed to the contents of the Underhill

wagon. It had been offloaded to make it somewhat easier to lift and place on wooden blocks until time to re-attach the new front axle.

A loud sigh escaped her lips. "Sometimes I wonder if we will *ever* reach Fort Hall," she said.

Willis limped over to the woman he had fallen in love with and gently touched her arm. "We will. I'm sure other trains have had problems like ours, and they persevered."

Elizabeth nodded, adding, "So many delays and summer is almost over. I just hope we get there before the first snows come."

"Those four men already have proven themselves to be heroes, in my book. They'll get us through."

She turned and gave Thigpen a weak smile before walking back to their wagon. Willis sighed heavily watching her.

The next morning, Roper called a few stout men to his side. "Need you men to lift that axle so we can slide the wheels on to see if they fit proper."

The Underhill boys were there to help. Roper turned to Clay and added, "You and Ernest grab a hold of that wheel and see if it fits. Me and Royce will do the right one."

He looked at Micah, Johan and James and declared, "You boys ready?"

"Anytime you are."

"On the count of three. One. Two. Three!"

Muscles bulged as the woodsmen hefted the green wood and held position.

The right one went on smoothly.

"Can't get it on, Mr. Roper," Clay grunted.

Newt skedaddled to the left wheel and examined it. "Gonna need to take a shave or two more off." He glanced at the three and grinned, "You boys all right?"

"Ya," grunted Johan.

"Pull that wheel, Royce," he ordered while helping Ernest and Clay remove and lay the heavy piece on the ground.

The axle quickly landed there too.

Picking up a chisel and wooden mallet, Newt began shaving the area where the hub would rest. When he was satisfied with his work, he said, "Let's try it again."

The men and boys took their places again. This time, both wheels fit and a cheer went up at the news.

"Let me get some holes started for the braces, then we'll be set." After measuring from the old axle, Roper picked up an auger and went to work. He signaled when he was finished. James and Johan carried the new one over to the wagon and slid it underneath.

"Gonna need you boys help again hoisting that axle up while I brace it into place," Roper informed.

Without a word, Lavanier and Svenson positioned themselves outside, lying on their backs ready to raise the green wood into place. Cunningham crawled underneath with Newt, also on their backs facing the underside of the bed.

Forty-five minutes later, four tired men crawled from under the wagon with broad grins. Shoulders were slapped for a job well done.

"Verlyn? You go fetch your ma and Mrs. Roper," Newt said. "Ernest and Clay? You help set things right in the wagon."

Mr. Roper turned to Micah and asked, "Think we ought to move out? It'd be nigh on supper afore we get things loaded back in Underhill's wagon."

"Morning will be soon enough."

"Suits me just fine," he said.

"Well, I see ya got it all done," Packy said, sidling up to Micah and Newt.

"Where the hell you been?" Micah asked, his voice saddled with disapproval.

"Who me?" Packy thumbed at his chest. "I… ah… was helping a few folks over yonder."

Cunningham snorted, "More'n likely, ya was sleeping

under a tree while the rest of us was workin'."

"Why you know me better'n that. I would a helped if'n I'd known."

Punching a finger into Woods chest, Micah smiled and said, "Oh, I know ya, Packy. Know ya too well." Then, he strode off shaking his head.

Scratching his own noggin, the lean woodsman, muttered, "Well, don't that beat all?"

Newt Roper snickered all the way back to his family.

Cunningham was unable to get comfortable. Usually he slept soundly, but not this night.

"Having trouble?" a voice whispered in the dark.

Recognizing Lavanier's soft baritone, Micah answered, "Yeah. Got an itching between my shoulder blades." He turned to look at his comrade and asked, "You?"

"Me too," James added, "Been watching the morning suns. Don't like what I'm seeing."

"Yep. Lot of mare's tails up there the last few days," Micah explained.

"Think Packy was right."

"How so?"

"He said this train was jinxed," James stated.

"Hush your mouth."

James chuckled. "Morning is gonna come early enough, best we both try for a little sleep."

"Aye."

The same red sky greeted them once again. Even the settlers marveled at the brilliant colors. The sunrise was as pretty as a redheaded vixen at Christmas.

Slurping the last of his coffee, James announced, "We best be moving. Should reach the Platte River by noon."

He and Micah shared a worried look but kept their thoughts silent.

Turning, Elizabeth smiled, "So, are we making good time?"

"Passable," the stout huntsman said.

Svenson's Swedish lilt bellowed down the line, "Wagon's ho!"

Teams heaved into their harnesses and trace chains rattled as the heavy wagons began to move. Ten in all fanned out behind the leader so not to constantly eat the dust drifting behind.

JP and others, now seasoned wranglers, kept the remuda and stock on a pace aligned with the homesteaders. Cows bawled their reluctance to move.

Laughter and happy chatter sprinkled the air as the pioneers began to envision the end of their long journey.

Packy was sent ahead to scout for a river crossing

Johan rode alongside the wagons.

Micah and James hung back, riding drag.

"Still got that itch running up and down your backbone?" James asked.

"Yep, and getting stronger," Micah replied. "You?"

"Same."

"Hope it ain't an early blizzard."

"It's happened before."

Micah nodded and added, "I know. These folks would never make it if that were the case."

"Remember the Donner Party?" James recalled.

"That never should have happened," Micah said flatly.

"Nope," James agreed, "But it did."

"Curtright would have led these folks to a similar demise, if we hadn't discovered JP."

"Afraid so."

Looking up, Micah noted, "Clouds building."

"No wind, neither."

"Might have a bit of a storm coming on us."

"Northwest."

"Yep."

Topping a gentle ridge, Packy reined up his dingy mule. What he saw made him eject a lung full of air. The Platte River lay below in all its glory. The sun's rays made the water sparkle like diamonds, scattered here and there across the plain as it meandered its determined course.

He didn't like what he saw to the northwest. A roiling, black behemoth of a cloud approached. It was a churning, bubbling cauldron. Silent streaks of lightning danced through its darkness every few seconds.

A chill tickled his spine, making him visibly shudder. He remembered overhearing Micah and James quietly discussing a premonition. He thought nothing of it at the time, but now it had come full circle.

"Those two fellas were right," he muttered to himself. "We're in for one hell of a ride."

Whirling the mule, he pushed it to run like the dickens before all hell broke loose.

It wasn't long until he slid to a stop next to Johan. Packy gulped air before he could report.

"What's got your britches all in a twist?" he asked.

"Where's Micah and James?" Packy asked.

Johan thumbed over his shoulder and said, "Drag."

Packy rammed heels into the mule's ribs, making it grunt, as he urged it to the back of the train.

Rounding in alongside his friends, he gasped for more air then exploded, "You two was right about them feelings you've been having."

James and Micah tossed stares back and forth, and then looked at Packy for explanation.

"What do you mean?"

Still sucking more wind into his deflated lungs, Woods explained, "Overheard ya talking 'bout a feeling ya been having."

"So?"

"It's 'bout to come true. Follow me," he added, spun the mule and took off.

Three men raced over the prairie to the gentle ridge, sliding their mounts to an abrupt stop when they saw the boiling monster in the sky.

"Holy Mother of God," whispered James.

"Ain't that the damn truth," answered Packy.

"Damn!" was all Micah could muster.

Working in sync for so long, the trappers knew without a word what needed to be done to save the wagon train.

Whirling and whipping their mounts, they sped back

to the procession. Johan's brow furrowed as he watched the frantic approach of his comrades. Concern filled his eyes as he waited.

As they slid to a stop next to him, he calmly asked, "Something's got yer britches' on fire. What is it, more Injuns?"

"Worse."

"Ya?"

"Platte's just over that ridge," Micah said.

"Good. I'm tired of playing nursemaid ta these greenhorns."

Ignoring Johan's comment, Micah announced, "We's walking right into the biggest storm any of us has ever seen."

"Ya?"

Packy's head bobbed as he squinted and added, "Yeah! Never seen clouds look meaner. These look like a herd of stampedin' buffs."

"What?"

"It's true," added James. "Ain't never seen the likes before."

Micah, impatient because their chatter was wasting precious time, butted in, "We ain't got time to be jawing. Gotta whip these teams up and get across the Platte before it hits."

He turned to Packy and said, "Find JP. Tell him to stampede that herd. The wagons will follow."

Spinning the roan, he bellowed down the line, "Whip 'em up! Move! Whip those teams!"

James and Johan echoed his call, urging wagon drivers to whip their teams into a full out run.

Taking the reins from Elizabeth, Thigpen yelled and snapped his whip over his team, urging them into a frightened run.

He spotted Micah and called out to him. Micah rode closer.

"What the hell is going on?"

"You'll see when ya top that ridge. Whip 'em harder, Thigpen!" he yelled as he rode away.

Willis did as he was told, pushing the team with everything they had.

"Mama? I'm scared," came a wail from inside the bouncing wagon.

Elizabeth turned in her seat, trying mightily not to be bounced out of the wagon and under the rampaging wheels. She called out to her daughters, saying, "Come closer and hang on to the back of the seat."

Topping the ridge, Thigpen's eyes bulged at what he saw, "Good Lord Almighty!"

Hearing his words, Elizabeth threw a look over her

shoulder, "Oh my God!"

"Mama what is it?" a frightened voice asked.

Mrs. Livingston's heart banged against her ribs like a barrel filled with rocks and spiraling downhill. Her stomach dropped to the soles of her shoes as she struggled to catch her breath.

"Mama?"

"A bad storm," she said, understating the danger and trying to reassure her girls.

She turned to Thigpen, "What are we going to do?"

"Do exactly what them boys tells us, that's what!"

Fighting to keep the teams in check as they raced down the sloping terrain, Thigpen brought the wagon to a stop on the banks of the river. Others did the same fanning out around the other wagons letting their teams blow and hack following the hard run.

The settlers were silent, each one eyeballing the churning black cloud with its intermittent veins of lightning. The ominous phenomena gave the illusion the end of the world approached.

"Oh, Mother of Mercy!" Elizabeth whispered, watching the clouds advance.

"Ain't never seen the like," replied Willis, softly.

CHAPTER 19

"James?" Micah called, reining his lathered roan next to the French-Canadian. "You know this river?"

"Somewhat."

"Know where we could get these wagons across?"

Lavanier studied the calm shallow looking water. His obsidian eyes followed the banks up and down trying to decern the best passage across. Finally, he pointed and said, "Down there. But have JP and Packy take the stock across first. Make sure it's solid bottom and there's no washed-out eddies we can't see. A wheel could sink into one and flip over."

"Right," Micah said and whirled his horse around. He headed for JP and Packy.

JP was mesmerized by the torrent that hovered on the horizon. "Oh, Lordy! I ain't never seen the likes of that, not even in Ohio," he whispered.

Cunningham approached at a gallop, flagging his arms

to draw their attention. "James reckons the best place to cross is down there," he declared, pointing and sucking in air. "Take the herd and cross them there. Look for hidden holes under the water. Once across, hurry back and help us get the wagons through."

The two sat staring at him.

"Move it! We ain't got much time. This thing's about to blow wide open!"

His warning jerked them out of their stupor.

JP called for his two wranglers, pointing and circling his arm in signal. Cunningham and Packy drove the herd from the rear.

"When they hit the water, watch to see if any stock seems to sink. It'll tell where a hole is," Micah yelled over the approaching din.

Packy nodded.

The cattle and horses hesitated for a few moments then plunged into the water, bawling their displeasure.

Woods kept his eyes peeled, watching the animals push through the stream to the other side. The stock's caterwauling drowned all sounds until they got to the other side of the Platte.

Driving them up the bank, Cunningham bellowed to the others, "Good job. Now, let's get back to the wagons!"

Taking the lead and splashing to the opposite bank. He raced to the Thigpen wagon and issued orders. "Willis, do you have the strength to drive your team across?"

Taking a deep breath, he replied, "I think so."

"Good man. Lead 'em out!"

Breathing deeply, Thigpen slapped rumps and the wagon rolled into the water.

Glimpsing Johan and James nearby, Micah pointed and ordered, "Spot Thigpen's wagon across!"

They waved approval and accompanied the wagon into the rolling water.

The moaning of the pending storm increased to a full-scale roar as the wind became a gale. In a few seconds, the air went from warm to frosty. Animals and humans alike were now exhaling puffs of fog because of the sudden drop of temperature.

Packy's head whipped around. He stared at the oncoming storm and announced, "Damn! This ain't gonna turn out well."

"No, it ain't," Micha said, motioning for the third wagon in line to cross. "Take charge of Mrs. Underhill's wagon. She and her boys can't handle this."

Micha was issuing orders as fast as the wind was whipping words from his mouth. Frantic in all the commotion, his roan kept whirling in circles. It was becoming more uncontrollable by the second.

Keeping an eagle eye on the approaching cataclysm, Micah could see sheets of rain approaching at an ungodly pace. "Roper! Lester! Whip 'em up!" he shouted.

Thunder, directly overhead, struck with such suddenness it caught man and animal off guard. Women screamed and horses panicked. Packy's mule almost tossed him to the ground.

It echoed through the valley. Before it could dissipate, the horizon turned fiery golden as a ball of lightning struck a distant cottonwood. It burst into flames as if it had been doused with coal oil.

Mother Nature was angry, and she had the wagon train in her sights.

A moment later, the torrential rain arrived and blindsided everyone, soaking humans and animals. The water fell from the heavens in buckets. Gallons of water spilled all at once.

The wagons pulled alongside each other entering the water. One horse reared on Lester's team, knocking another down. It squealed in despair as it tried to regain its footing and keep from drowning. Finally, it stood, shaking and spraying water.

Whirling the roan, Cunningham rode into the fray. He flew out of his saddle and swam toward the destressed team. Grabbing the collar of one he scrambled aboard the back of the team. Pulling the slack reins, he spoke calmly and nudged them forward with his heels.

When they reached high ground, he hopped off and ordered Lester to clear the area for the last two wagons. He sprinted to his roan, mounted and charged back into the raging waters.

Intent on reaching the other side as quickly as possible, Micah didn't hear or see the wall of water that hit him broadside. Charging down from the mountains, where the storm amassed its fury, the raging torrent flung him and his horse into a boiling cauldron of debris and destruction.

Stunned, Svenson and Lavanier didn't know what to do first. Should they try to rescue their friend or stay with the homesteaders.

Barely able to see, Johan and James charged through the lashing rain, in search of Micah. They stayed as close to the edge as they dared. They could be unknowingly sucked into the current because the soil was collapsing from the rush of water. Desperate for a glimpse of Micah bobbing in the thrashing river, the effort was futile. The turbulent waters and pouring rain was too intense; it all but obscured their vision. Their hearts sank as they gave in and returned to the two wagons left on their side of the Platte.

The settlers stared in disbelief as the debris filled wall of water slammed into Cunningham, submerging him and his horse in the roiling current. Voices got caught in throats. Startled onlookers were unable to respond to the possible loss of one of their beloved leaders. Man and horse simply disappeared under the foaming lather.

Tears sprang from Packy's eyes, as he ran along the bank, his eyes frantically searching for his friend. His voice screeched against the howl of the river and wind. Breathless, he sagged to his knees and lifted his closed eyes to the pouring rain. The cacophony of Mother Nature drowned out his anguished call to the best friend he ever had.

He didn't know how long he had remained there, just that his teeth were chattering from the cold. It was his icy leather clothes that brought him back. He stood, turned and ran back to the wagons and settlers who needed his help.

Abruptly Packy stopped. The thrashing of rushing water was the only sound because the wind had silenced. He looked up to see big, fat snowflakes falling. They were beginning to litter the ground and cover it quickly. He stepped up his pace.

CHAPTER  20

Micha was being tossed under the water like a ragdoll. He didn't know which way was up or down. He ricocheted off logs and other hidden objects. He felt his face scrape the rocky bottom at one point. The pain alerted him he was still alive. He tried to open his eyes, but all he saw was murky brown sludge. So, he shut them and pushed off the bottom in an effort to get back to the top of the raging river.

His starving lungs gobbled a load of air before he was dragged to the bottom again. He rolled and tumbled in the water's turbulent thrust. He didn't fight it but did his best to protect his head.

His lungs felt as if they would explode. He gathered what strength he could and pushed off the bottom, clawing his way back to the surface.

As he struggled to keep his head above water and gobble air, something struck his shoulder hard. He reached back and hugged a log to his torso. Waves still washed over his head, but the timber he hugged kept him afloat so he could feed his weary lungs. The more air he sucked, the more cognizant he became of his surroundings. The bank was only a few yards away.

Using the buoyancy of the log, he kicked and propelled himself to land. When his feet struck firm ground, he stood but his legs buckled against the rushing torrent. Using the log for support, he fought his way closer to the shore. His legs felt like he was dragging a heavy ball and chain. Reaching the bank, he clawed himself onto soggy soil.

He rested briefly and resumed his desperate battle against the elements, crawling ten yards at a time. When he got to tall prairie grass that was not covered in water, he crumpled from total exhaustion. Then, everything went black.

The quiet was deafening to Packy's ears after the tumultuous storm. He continued to walk toward the pioneers. The only noise he could hear was the slight shushing sound of fresh snow under his feet.

The settlers stood silently, watching him approach. Elizabeth saw the grief etched across his face. His eyes were filled with deep pain. She touched his arm drawing him out of his morass.

"I am so sorry, Mr. Woods," she said.

Drawing a deep shaky breath, Packy nodded. No words could express his anguish.

Noticing his blue lips, she strode back to their wagon

and retrieved a blanket for him.

He gratefully accepted it, pulling it around his shoulders.

Thigpen stepped forward and asked, "What should we do now?"

Blinking, Packy had to gather his thoughts before answering. "Make camp," he said, glancing around and pointing. "Circle the wagons over there and get some fires going so we all can warm up and dry out. Tonight, will be colder."

"After that downpour? How do you expect us to find dry wood?" someone tossed out.

Anger erupted from the sorrowful woodsman. He had lost patience with the greenhorns.

"Why everyone knows to keep dry tinder in ya wagon, ya numbskull!" he barked.

Surprised by his outburst, Packy's eyes quickly canvassed the homesteaders. They still weren't moving. "Circle the dang wagons!" he shouted.

Heavy, wet snow covered the soaked ground quickly. It was piled three inches deep and still accumulating. James and Johan kept riding the bank. hoping their friend, Micah, had survived the flash flood. They saw no sign of him.

The abrupt change in weather meant they were facing

a freezing night ahead. No one was prepared for it. They had no way of telling how much snow might fall or when it would warm up again, if ever. In the back of their minds, they suspected winter may have arrived early, and they were still two or three weeks out of Fort Hall. That knowledge did not sit well. Driving wagons through snowpack was no fun.

The river was still flowing too high and too fast for the last two families to cross.

The dark clouds blocked the sun and darkness arrived earlier than usual. The two huntsmen discontinued their search and headed back to wagon train and its hapless settlers.

Neither one spoke of their loss. Their grief was enormous and the loss of their friend dampened their spirit.

When they arrived the two families already had set up a small camp, with a tarp to keep the snow off and a small fire that provided heat.

Somberly, the men dismounted and stripped the tack from their horses. They dropped it under the makeshift shelter and wrapped their saddle blankets around their shoulders.

"Any luck?" Sam Peters asked.

Still numb, the woodsmen could not muster an answer. They just shook their head.

Peters' wife, Abagail, handed them steaming cups of

coffee, and said, "I'm sorry for your loss. Mr. Cunningham was a good man."

James savored the hot liquid relishing the warmth coursing through his chilled insides. "Yessum, he was."

"Ya, won't never find another like him," Johan added, taking a plate of food that was offered.

Clearing his throat, Will Taggert asked, "How long you boys known each other?"

James and Johan cut a short look at each other. Thinking on the question, James answered first.

"Don't rightly know," he said.

"You don't?"

"Ya, time means nothing to us," Johan ventured, "When the snow melt happens, we take furs into Trader Charley's post in Sinking Springs. Summer and fall we work on traps, getting them ready fer winter. That's all we know."

"A simple life," Abagail said with a smile.

"And a good one," added James.

"Well, we are mighty obliged you all came along when you did," Taggert said.

Nodding, Svenson remarked, "Ya, none of yins would have made it to Fort Hall the way Curtright was doing ya."

Murmurs of agreement floated in the cold air.

"Best we all get some sleep and try to stay warm," suggested James. "We'll see what tomorrow brings."

"Ya, pray for a better tomorrow."

Slowly, Micah Cunningham rose from the depths of exhaustion, gradually becoming aware of his surroundings. His ears picked up a smothered silence his muddled brain thought odd. He wasn't sure he was alive or dead.

Keeping his eyes closed, he flexed his hands. He smiled because they worked. Next, he wiggled his toes and twisted his ankles. Those moved without discomfort, too.

Opening his eyes, he had to blink several times to bring back the focus. All they saw was pitch blackness. He realized he was spread-eagled and lying on his back. He tried to sit up, but pain sliced through him like an icy dagger that left him breathless.

Resuming his prone position, he let his mind slowly wrap around the events that left him lying where he was. He closed his eyes, and his mind revisited the storm. He had been trying to get the settlers across the Platte to safety when a wall of water slammed into he and his horse. They were submerged in its powerful wake. The thought of almost drowning sucked the wind out of his lungs and sent his heart to pounding.

He breathed deeply, calming the sudden panic and turned his thoughts elsewhere. Opening his eyes, he stared into the darkness. He had no idea how far downstream the current had taken him. He had lost a good horse. his gear and a Hawken rifle. His hand touched where his Bowie would normally be. It also was gone.

Rolling to his side he gingerly sat up. He was surprised to see himself covered with several inches of heavy, wet snow. He was sore everywhere from the beating his body took underwater. He raked a hand through his hair feeling the hard particles of ice clinging to the curls. When he stroked his unruly beard, it, too, was frozen.

Suddenly, his numb mind and body reacted to the cold that slammed into him from out of nowhere. Frozen to the core, he began shivering uncontrollably.

Staggering to his full height, Cunningham began the trek back to his friends and the wagon train. He hoped he was heading in the right direction. Ice broke from his frozen leathers with each step he took, but his body movement generated some heat.

CHAPTER

Dawn opened under thick pewter skies, revealing a gray and white canvas. The only color was the wagons scattered about with tendrils of smoke rising from small fires in the windless air. A misty frozen vapor hung over the land. Puffs of fog accented each word the settlers spoke. Their voices were subdued. The previous day's events had shredded the settlers' resolve. They all would remember the events for months to come.

Many were bundled in so many layers of clothing they could barely move about doing morning chores.

Six inches of fresh snow, wet and heavy, dotted the landscape as far as the eye could see. The air was bitter cold, reminding everyone winter was not far off and they still had many miles to travel to reach their destination.

Packy had walked down to the river's edge to stare across at the two wagons which had yet to cross. Debris littered the banks, but the water was still too high and fast to ford safely. He didn't see Johan and James. He wondered if they might be looking for Micah. He exhaled loudly, knowing in his gut they would never find him. Turning, he walked back to Thigpen's camp.

Taking the coffee offered, he guzzled the hot brew with the hope it would chase the chill he felt inside.

Stepping closer, Thigpen asked, "How's the river?"

"Well, we got wood to burn if the kids want to drag some here."

"JP could gather the youngsters for that. We could all do with a roaring fire to warm us."

"I won't argue with that," Packy agreed, "River is still too high and moving too fast to bring the other two wagons across."

"How long for it to subside?"

Packy shrugged, draining his coffee, and refilling the cup. Straightening from the fire, he focused on Thigpen. "Can't rightly say. But if I was a bettin' man, tomorrow or the next day be more'n likely."

Willis nodded. "Did you see James and Johan on the other side?"

Shaking his head, Packy said, "Not right off."

"Think they could be looking for Mr. Cunningham?" piped up JP.

Sipping air, Packy didn't want to damage JP's hope for the robust woodsman's return, but he opted for the truth. He looked at him sorrowfully and said, "Doubt they will find him, boy. Ain't never seen a wall of water like that come down a river. Hope to never see it again, too."

He drained the cup, set it down and walked off. JP looked at his father with questioning eyes. Willis smiled weakly and said, "Why don't you gather the other kids and bring us some firewood."

Dropping his head, JP nodded and went to round up the others, his feet dragging in the snow and showing his despair over losing a good friend.

Reining their horses alongside each other, Lavanier and Svenson sat the leather gloomily. They stared at the still muddy but turbulent water. They were about a mile down from the two wagons on their side of the river.

"If he made it to the shore and crawled into the grass, his buckskins would make him impossible to see," James reasoned.

"Ya, could be buried under six inches of snow, too."

"He would have been soaked to the bone. A man could easily freeze to death."

"Ya. That's a problem."

"See any sign of his roan?" James asked.

Johan shook his head.

James signed heartily and exhaled a long, foggy breath before adding, "Not much more we can do."

"River's not safe to cross yet."

"Maybe tomorrow."

"Hope so," added Johan.

Wheeling their mounts around, they rode back to the makeshift camp.

The flotsam from the riverbank, delivered to each wagon by the kids, made for smoky fires. The wet wood slowly was drying out and producing heat for the cold and weary travelers.

Woods was lost without his friend, Micah. The land still was open and free, but good friends were seldom found. Trying to keep them was harder. The lanky woodsman was not one to lead others. Now, he was thrust into that position because Micah had been swept away.

"Hey, Woods!" Adolph Geller called out as he approached. Puffs of fog accented his heavy breathing and matched his stride in the snow.

Packy turned when he heard the German's thick accent and watched the short, stocky man walk toward him.

"Yeah?" he replied.

"We leaving soon?" he asked, his face hopeful.

Shaking his head, "No. Gotta, wait for the other two wagons."

"Why? We already got hit by one snowstorm. How many others 'til Fort Hall?"

Short of patience, Packy yelled, "You don't listen none too good! We wait fer the river ta go down, then we move." He spit and pointing, "Now, get back to ya camp!"

"Yao der du werde uus toten!" Adolph shouted.

"Huh?"

Geller translated, spittle flying from his angry lips, "You gonna kill us!"

Willis Thigpen entered the fray. "Mr. Geller? We need to abide by these men's commands. They know what they are doing; we don't."

"Ya, der blinde führt den blinden!" he mumbled, stalking off.

Turning, Packy looked at Thigpen and shook his said. "What'd he say?" he asked.

Elizabeth stepped closer, "I think he said something about the blind leading the blind."

"You know his words?"

She smiled and said, "Some."

Exhaling a huge sigh, Packy watched the German return to his family's campfire, arms flailing and gibberish escaping his mouth.

"Well, nothing we can do 'bout the weather, except hunker down and wait," the reluctant leader said.

Reaching for the pot, Elizabeth asked, "More coffee?"

"Yes ma'am."

Stopping to catch his breath, Micah kept moving, resisting the urge to lay down in the snow and rest. Doing so, he knew would be certain death. He wasn't ready to give up; he wouldn't surrender just yet.

He was still following the river. Carefully, he rechecked his bearings. The gray sky was lighter in one direction giving way to the probability that was east. He stared at the river for a few moments. It was still turbulent. Besides, he wasn't all that anxious to get soaked, again, He was still chilled to the bone. Walking had warmed him up but not enough to stop the shivering. The cold had penetrated every cell and fiber of his being. His robust health was the only thing keeping him alive.

Tearing his eyes away from the river, Micah turned to his left and kept walking.

Rays of sunshine broke through the gray cloudbank. The wind was picking up, helping to blow the overcast skies to the south. Shimmering light hit the snow and shattered it into millions of diamonds.

198

Packy marveled at the sight. "Well now, ain't that pretty," he exclaimed as he stepped from under the makeshift shelter.

"Reminds me of Pennsylvania after a bad storm," Mrs. Livingston said softly, standing at Packy's elbow.

Looking at her he grinned, "We get some damn... Oops, sorry ma'am."

She looked at her snow-covered shoes and hid her amusement.

"What I meant to say, is we get some powerful storms in the Rockies. Afterward, the plumb beauty of it can take ya breath away."

"I can imagine," she said with smile.

Noticing Packy and Mrs. Livingston standing away from their camp, Lavanier called out from the other side of the river. He waved and shouted, "Hey, Packy!"

After conversing for a few moments, James announced, "We're coming over."

"I wouldn't just yet," The skinny woodsman replied. "Looks a little too high."

Ignoring Woods, the men mounted and gingerly urged their horses into the swirling current.

Belly-high water forced them to pull their legs out of the stirrups and hold them up higher. When they safely reached the other side, they were smiling.

"Belly-high is still too high for them two wagons over there," Woods commented. "They'd be floating."

"Ya, tomorrow we cross," added Johan.

"Good. Got a few complainin' on the delay," Packy added and nodded toward the pioneers who were gathered around warming fires, "Be glad when we get shuck of these folks and get back to what we came here ta do in the first place, huntin' buffs."

"Do ya not like these folks?" Johan asked.

"Well, some of them, I do."

"Damned if Mushy ain't already come and gone," James teased.

Packy gave him a cockeyed look and was about to hurl an insult his way when Thigpen's voice called out, "You boys want some coffee?"

"Ya, that be nice."

"Come ahead," answered Willis, waving them closer to the fire."

Stumbling over an unseen object, Micah crashed to the ground. He groaned but mustered the strength to roll over on his back. Exhaustion overwhelmed him. He closed his eyes and drifted off.

Something deep inside pulled him from his bliss. He

awoke suddenly, instantly aware of his surroundings.

His ears perked.

He held his breath.

He feared moving a muscle would muffle the sound.

He closed his eyes and concentrated on the sounds, the noises beyond the rushing water. It was faint, but he definitely could decern voices slithering on wind.

His heart surged.

He gasped with unfounded joy.

The boisterous laugh that filled the air was familiar. It was that of the big Swede.

"I'm so close, but so far…" he whispered to himself..

Opening his eyes, he forced his body to move. His mind finally won over his body. He rolled onto his side. Again, he was lying in fresh, unmarked snow.

Worn and exhausted, he pulled his elbows under him and propped his head up. Next, he pulled his knees up and tried to balance. He was too weak. He crashed on to his backside, where he stayed and sucked in huge gulps of air.

He was so cold. It felt like he was wrapped in a blanket of ice.

His head drooped.

Again, his eyes closed.

Unable to keep his balance, he flopped sideways and

passed out in the snow again.

Willpower forced his eyes to open one more time.

Micah knew he was in the last moments of life. Death seemed to be calling him to the false security of its warm cocoon. He refused to give in.

Concentrating on one arm, he forced it to rise and flop against the snow. A leg was next. He kept repeating the motions until he was fully awake.

His teeth chattered like a magpie.

Taking a deep breath, he sat up. Gradually crawled on his knees and slowly pushed himself upright. Swaying slightly, Micah began the arduous task of placing one foot in front of the other, heading in the direction of the voices.

Could he make it?

CHAPTER  22

Dusk had fallen beneath a clear sky. There was little wind but the temperatures was dropping fast. Johan and James had gone back across the river to inform the Taggert and Peters families they would be moving out in the morning.

JP had gone to gather more firewood. His shoes broke the icy crust with every step. His arms loaded; JP abruptly halted when he heard crunching sounds much like his own. They sounded like footsteps that were moving parallel to his own but along the water's edge. His head swiveled to the left from where he heard the noise.

Suddenly, the crunching sound of footsteps was accompanied by heavy breathing.

Fear began climbing up his spine. He couldn't yell; his voice was frozen in his throat.

JP couldn't move. His were feet rooted to the ground like a sturdy oak. All sorts of things swirled through his young brain. Was he being stalked by a wild creature of some sort, a wolf perhaps? He had no idea what it could be.

What he saw sent a surge of energy through his limbs.

He tossed the wood into the air and run quickly back to his camp, yelling, "Pa! Pa!"

Hearing the frightened voice, Thigpen and Packy rushed to the edge of the makeshift camp.

Sliding to a stop in front of his father, eyes big as saucers, JP pointed and shouted, "Pa! Something's out there. It came out of the river walking on two legs!"

Elizabeth quickly gathered her daughters and hustled them into the wagon.

"Stay put and not a peep. You hear me?" she whispered.

Two heads bobbed in unison.

Looking around, she found the Hawken rifle and pulled it from its resting place. She rushed to Willis' side and handed him the rifle.

Packy immediately raced to the river.

Resting a hand on his son's shoulder, Willis asked, "Was it human?"

Eyes still wide with fright, JP yelled, "No, but the creature was walking upright."

Gripping the rifle firmly in his hand, Thigpen followed Packy into the darkness.

Spotting the prone figure, Woods approached slowly studying the form lying face down in the snow. Apprehensively, he grabbed an arm and flipped the stranger on its back. Stunned, he yelled, "It's Micah! He's alive!"

Thigpen limped hurriedly to Packy's side. Recognizing the face, he knelt touching Micah's cheek. "Lordy! He's half frozen," Thigpen said. "JP, bring me a blanket. Quick!"

"We need Johan and James to carry him," Packy rose and raced to the river's edge. Cupping hands around his mouth to carry the sound further, he shouted, "James? Johan? Come quick. It's Micah!" Then, he spun and raced back to his friend.

The woodsmen cut a sharp glance at each other. James frowned and Johan asked, "What's he blathering about now?"

"Think he said something about Micha."

Realization hit them suddenly. They dropped their coffee cups and bolted from the camp. They leaped atop their horses and rode bareback across the river. The Peters and Taggert families were stunned by the speed in which the two men moved. Curiosity pulled them to the edge of the river, but they could see nothing in the darkness. They returned to their warm fires, knowing whatever was happening on the other side would be revealed to them sooner or later.

The hunters splashed across the stream and dismounted on the fly alongside Packy and Thigpen.

"I'll be damned…" whispered James, kneeling next to

the prone huntsman. "We need to get him thawed out."

The burly Svenson shoved everyone aside, went down on one knee and gathered the unconscious Cunningham in his arms. A grunt escaped his lips as he rose. Micah weighed almost as much as the Swede.

The group headed back toward the Thigpen's fire. Willis called out to his son long before they arrived.

"JP? More wood! On the double!" he said.

The youth did as he was instructed, gathering everything he had dropped moments earlier

"Elizabeth, we need a good warm bed made, please?" Thigpen shouted.

Running to the back of the wagon Mrs. Livingston ordered her daughters, "I need all the blankets and quilts. Quickly now, girls."

"Yes, Mama." The items were gathered and tossed to their mother.

Taking them, Elizabeth made a bed as close to the fire as she dared. She strained her eyes on the darkness as the men approached with Cunningham.

Stooping to let his tall frame clear the low hanging tarp, Svenson stepped toward the makeshift bed and laid his friend down gently and backed away. He was breathing heavily after carting Micha from the riverbank. His eyes were filled with wonder, though.

Elizabeth was shocked by the sight of the frozen frontiersman. She knelt at his side and covered him with the quilts and blankets. She tucked them tightly about his limbs for warmth.

"My goodness," she exclaimed. "His hair and beard are full of ice."

Livingston ran her fingers through his hair, trying to dislodge the frozen particles.

"JP, throw more wood on that fire, will ya?" James asked.

"Yes, sir," he replied, gradually adding larger pieces.

Everyone was silenced by the miracle of Micah's return and the fortitude it must have taken to survive such an ordeal. The only sound was moisture sizzling as the flames ate the wet wood. Everyone waited for him to thaw and open his eyes.

His condition unchanged, James knelt by the Scotch-Irishman, reached under the layers and touched Micah's hand. It was stone cold.

"He's not warming up," James exclaimed.

"What do we do?" asked Packy.

"We gotta warm his body up, or he won't make it," conceded James.

Something flickered in Elizabeth's brain. She looked at the men and said, "I have an idea." Then, she turned and ran to the back of the wagon.

No one had any idea what the widow had up her sleeve, but they watched intently.

Leaning out the back of the wagon, she called, "Willis? Come take these."

When he arrived, she handed three pots to him.

"Fill these with coals and place them around his body."

Thigpen gave her a questioning look.

"They'll be bed warmers!" she smiled. Thigpen helped her down from the wagon and the two raced back to the patient. The frontiersmen looked at her as if she had lost her mind. Undaunted, Elizabeth clapped her hands and issued orders, "Hurry now. Fill these pots with coals."

They scrambled to do her bidding. Handing the filled pots to her, Elizabeth placed the warm pots as close to Micah as she could without burning him. Then she explained.

"The pots will create the heat his body needs. The covers will keep it nice and toasty under there."

Again, they looked at her with doubt. She shook her head and said, "What? You never heard of bed warmers?"

"Um, no ma'am," replied Packy.

"Well, now you have," she said, turned to her girls and

ordered them to bed.

"Aww, Mama! We want to stay and make sure Mr. Cunningham wakes up."

She pointed and demanded, "To bed, both of you."

"But Mama…"

"Scoot!" she said, glancing over her shoulder and adding, "Night, gentlemen."

A chorus sounded, "Night, Mrs. Livingston."

The men tossed quick glances at each other. Finally, James said what everyone was thinking.

"Can't do much more. We might as well rest also," he said and shrugged his shoulders.

Murmurs of agreement were heard as all settled down for a restless night of sleep beside the fallen leader.

CHAPTER  23

Rising from the depths of exhaustion and cold, the haze of unconsciousness slowly lifted, and Micah stirred. He still was too tired to open his eyes, but his nose twitched, picking up the familiar scent of woodsmoke. But there was something else.

He sniffed. His mind slowly began to awaken.

He sniffed again. Mixed in the smell of wood smoking, was the distinctive aroma of burnt leather. His foggy mind didn't understand.

What the hell? Where's that smell coming from?

Basking in his warm cocoon, the thought soon drifted away, and so did he. The darkness and warmth was too comforting.

Rising once again from the deep abyss, Cunningham forced his eyes to open. Blinking to bring them into focus, he realized he was laying on his back beneath a canvas ceiling. He lay still in the blackness and allowed his ears to identify his surroundings.

He concentrated on the sounds. There was the slight

crackling and popping of a nearby fire. There was muffled snoring, too. It was eerily quiet. No wind rustled. No horses stamped. His brow furrowed in response.

His mind worked overtime trying to grasp his situation. He couldn't remember what had happened. The mystery slammed into his gut and sucked the breath from his lungs.

Slowly, he calmed the panic, searching to recapture his focus. His nose wiggled. Again, he smelled something burning, but he could not recognize the scent..

What is that?

He sniffed again. It smelled faintly like smoldering hides and moldy blankets. He inhaled deeply, and suddenly he felt something burning his skin. His eyes flew open.

Micah lifted his head and noticed it was his covers that were smoking. Instantly, his eyes bulged, and he yelled. Frantically, he scrambled to break free of the cumbersome load of blankets on him. Whichever way he moved something hot seared his skin. With what little strength he had, he fought to untangle himself.

Finally, he burst free of the blankets, heaving them into the air and as far away as he could. Immediately, he spotted the covered pots. He grabbed a lid but dropped it quickly as the metal burned his fingers. Red, orange and gold embers were still glowing inside.

When he glanced wildly about, his eyes came to rest

on his comrades. They sat blinking and trying to clear the fog from their sleepy minds. They all thought the same thing.

Is Micah standing up or am I dreaming.

Micah's blue eyes stabbed the men staring at him. "What the hell ya trying ta do? Roast me alive?" He swatted at his smoking sleeve, then his britches.

Johan let loose with a wry grin, "I do believe our Micah has risen from the dead."

"Ain't that the dad-blamed truth," Packy added.

"And with all the bluff and bluster of a true mountain man," James proclaimed with a big smile.

The commotion roused Elizabeth from a sound sleep, and she peeked around the bonnet of the wagon. Her facial expression dulled by heavy sleep, but she smiled when she saw Micah standing.

The man everyone thought had died blasted the air with his deep baritone voice. He was hot and angry.

"Like hell!" he said, scouring the group with eyes ablaze, "Whose idea was this anyway? Who thought it would be a good idea to roast me to death!"

Elizabeth stepped forward and confessed, "It was mine, Mr. Cunningham." She pulled her cloak tighter to ward off the early morning chill and looked away. She suddenly felt guilty for saving his life.

"Why?" Micah screeched and whirled.

James rose, stepping closer to his friend. "Well, it's like this. Ya see…"

Flashing his eyes toward his ebony friend, Micah growled, "Like what?"

"Well, you was planning ta make the trip down the rabbit hole, ya see."

"What rabbit hole?" Micah asked angrily.

"Tis an old way of saying you was at death's door, partner," James explained.

"I was not!" Micah bellowed.

JP, Marah and Colleen's eyes were as big as wheel hubs, listening to the exchange.

"Mr. Cunningham!" Elizabeth shouted.

Still angry, Micah spun and stared at who had done everything possible to save his life. He had never heard her raise her voice before. "What?" he yelled back.

Elizabeth took a deep breath and glared right back at the outraged woodsman.

"If you would stop interrupting and being so belligerent, we are trying to explain this to you," she spat.

Her words gave him pause. Realizing he was hotter than the dad-blamed blankets, he took a deep breath and decided to listen.

Grins plastered the faces of his comrades at how quickly Mrs. Livingston had put the Scotch-Irishman in his place.

She tilted her head and smiled as if he were a child caught with his hand in the cookie jar. Then, she asked sharply, "Are you ready to listen, now?"

The brute took a deep breath, stepped back with his arms folded across his thick chest and waited. He allowed his head to rear back a tad, blue eyes studying her with trepidation before he consented and said, "Go ahead."

"Thank you," she said.

Livingston picked up a few sticks of wood and stoked the fire as she gathered her thoughts. When her eyes again looked at the angry man, she said softly, "You were dying, Mr. Cunningham. You had no more heat left in your body after being so wet and cold for so long."

Micah dropped his gaze.

"We had to do something to save you," she continued, "Bed warmers have been used for ages, and I thought they just might do the trick and warm you up. You were unconscious, and I wasn't gonna let that cold river claim you."

"And, boy, did your wake up!" chortled Packy, slapping his leg with pure joy.

"Oh shad-up, ya skinny hunk of hide," barked Micah.

Snickers of laughter flowed.

214

Turning back to Mrs. Livingston, Micah offered up, "Begging your pardon ma'am. I am humbled and much obliged for your forethought in saving my life."

"Apology accepted, Mr. Cunningham."

His glance slid to his friends, to whom he also offered thanks, "Same to y'all, too."

Johan stood and wrapped arms around Micah in a bear hug.

The Scotch-Irishman grunted from the pressure of the gesture. The big Swede didn't even notice. He slapped his friend's back with powerful thumps. As a results, Cunningham had to grapple for balance from the blows.

"Ya, right proud ya decided to come back ta the family," Svenson roared with happiness.

Grinning sheepishly, Micah answered, "Yeah, me too."

The sun's rays sparkled against the snow like pearl dust as the wagon train prepared to resume its journey. The last two wagons crossed the river without incident. The Peters and Taggert families were greeted warmly in the frosty air.

Standing off to the side, Micah and James watched the short reunion before the wagons began the trek to South Pass.

"Gonna have to pick a new mount from the remuda,"

James said.

"Not looking forward to it." Micah replied. "That roan was a good horse."

"Pick a Hawken from the Bailey's wagon if ya want."

"I will."

"The Underhill wagon has an extra saddle, I think," James added.

"They might."

Slanting a look at the stalwart mountain man, Lavanier smiled and said, "Better get your arse in gear, then. We'll be moving out shortly."

He turned and walked away, a sign everything was back to normal. Micha watched him strut off and let a smile slide across his features. It was good to be back.

After the near disaster at the river crossing — powerful rain, a torrent of rushing water and a freak snowstorm — the pioneers were longing for a respite from the previous tribulations.

The train rolled along at a steady pace. The mood was lighthearted and jovial. Happy chatter was evident from morning to night.

Packy Woods still kept his fingers crossed behind his back.

The itching between Lavanier's shoulder blades had eased somewhat but was still there.

Micah was adjusting to his new mount and the greenhorns he escorted. He still had reservations about them.

Svenson kept his jovial mindset but was on high alert. His eyes darted across the horizon, constantly surveying the terrain for anything or anyone who might cross their path.

They stopped at dusk after traveling a good distance. The woodsmen gathered around the Thigpen fire and enjoyed a hot meal, prepared by Mrs. Livingston. When they finished, everyone sat quietly smoking pipes and sipping coffee.

JP, Marah and Colleen had their ears perked for when the tales would start spewing from the huntsmen's mouths.

Thigpen broke the comfortable silence.

"Mr. Lavanier? When will we cross South Pass?" he asked.

"Already did."

"We did?"

"Yep, right before we set up camp tonight," James replied.

"Didn't look like a pass."

"We're at the bottom of the Great Divide," he said and took another sip of coffee. "That's a two-legged trek to cross the mountains further north. With your heavy wagons, this is the quickest and safest route."

"Curtright talked about taking the Hastings Cutoff if we got delayed much more. You know anything about that?" Willis asked.

The four men cut a short glance at each other.

"Then for sure, it's a good thing we saw JP," Packy voiced.

"That takes you off of what they call the California Trail," James said. "You folks be going to Oregon."

"Y'all never woulda made it, if Curtright had sent you down to Hastings," Johan added.

"Why?" asked JP.

"Death march," chimed in Micah.

Elizabeth turned, "Why do you say that?"

"Because that's what it would have turned into."

Her brow furrowed and she asked, "How?"

"Ya ever hear of the Donner Party debacle?"

She frowned, searched her memory and said, "Not sure."

Willis shook his head, "Me either."

The men fell silent, tossing looks at one another.

JP leaned forward, "Tell us, please?"

"It's not pretty," Micah replied.

"It will make your skin crawl," added Packy, his head bobbing briskly.

"Well, then tell us."

"Yins may get nary a wink of sleep, just thinking 'bout those poor souls," warned Johan.

"That bad, huh?" Willis questioned.

"That ain't the half of it," commented Packy."

"James here, knows more about it than the rest of us," Micah said, tossing the mantle to the French-Canadian.

Lavanier threw a dirty look at Cunningham.

All eyes drifted to the ebony-colored man. All waited with bated breath.

Pouring more coffee all around, Elizabeth asked James, "Were you there?"

"No. I was part of the rescue party, though," James said.

"And?"

"And it was something I never want to see again."

The kids were jiggling with excitement. "Tell us, please?" they chorused.

Packy offered up his two-cents worth to James, "You can leave out all the gory details."

James gave the skinny hide-hunter a scathing gaze.

Elizabeth gasped. "Gory?"

"Yes ma'am," he said, "Ya see, they was all starving, so they killed the weakest and ate their flesh."

Mrs. Livingstons' face blanched to the color of rice powder. She abruptly sat on a box, hand resting on her bosom and gasped for air.

"Shad-up, Packy!" hissed Micah. "You're gonna scare ten years growth outta these kids and everyone else."

"I ain't scared," piped up JP.

Finding her voice, Elizabeth eyes roamed the faces of the four mountain men and said, "Surely, you jest?"

Reluctantly stepping into the conversation, James answered, "I wish I was, Mrs. Livingston."

"Is that why you boys were so dead set against Curtright? Did you think he might pull a similar stunt?" Willis asked.

"May have been in the back of our minds," admitted Micah.

"I see…"

Impatient, JP asked, "You gonna tell the story or not?"

James stalled, sipped his coffee and said, "I think it's best you go roll up in those blankets. We got another long haul tomorrow."

"Aww, Mr. Lavanier!" JP lamented.

Relieved, Elizabeth stood and ushered her daughters to the wagon. "Let's go, girls. Off to bed."

Turning, she looked at the four woodsmen and mouthed, "Thank you."

They nodded in acknowledgement because none of them wanted to rehash details of the disastrous Donner Party.

CHAPTER  24

Expertly guiding his four-up after long months on the trail, Willis Thigpen sat easy on the seat with Elizabeth in comfortable silence.

JP was with the remuda and Marah and Colleen were sitting in the wagon looking out the back.

A weak fall sun was shining, broken occasionally by puffs of clouds floating across an azure sky. The treeless terrain was dotted with soft rolling hills and short valleys. It was accented by odd ridges that rose from nowhere. The dried grass was brown and waved in a constant wind, which carried a cool but fresh scent. The Rocky Mountains, snowcapped in the higher elevations, cast majestic shadows across the landscape.

They had become immune to the sounds of travel, hooves hitting thick turf, trace chains rattling, bonnets flapping to the wind and wheels squeaking their steady progress.

Licking dry lips, Willis mulled over how he would propose marriage to Elizabeth. After sharing space for months, he could not imagine starting over without her at his side.

"James said only two more days to Fort Hall," he said, sliding his eyes in her direction for a moment. "What are your plans?"

Elizabeth's heart plummeted to the worn soles of her high-top shoes. She didn't know what to say. The Thigpens had become part of her life, and she couldn't imagine going on without them.

Taking a deep breath, Willis took the plunge, "Since you and the girls joined me and JP, it seems to me we've kinda become a ready-made family," he said, testing the water.

Gazing straight ahead to disguise the rapid pounding of her heart, Elizabeth pursed her lips and smiled.

Is he suggesting what I think he's suggesting?

Not one to mince words, she turned to him and blurted out, "If ya be dangling a marriage proposal in front of my nose, Mr. Thigpen, I accept."

Willis still was focused on his own thoughts, concerned over separating from Elizabeth and her girls as their destination neared. He didn't hear a word she said. So, he added, "Of course, I'm sure you'd be a fine catch for any man hunting a wife."

"Mr. Thigpen?"

His head swiveled, "What?"

"I said, I accept."

Bumfuzzled, Willis' eyes grew wide and he asked, "Accept? What?"

She smiled at his confusion, "Willis, were you not asking me to marry you in a meandering sort of way?"

Thigpen was dumbstruck. She had picked through his ramblings and zeroed in on his intent. Sheepishly, he replied, "Um, yes. I guess I was asking for your hand in marriage."

"I accept."

"You do?"

Tilting her head, her face beamed. "The five of us have become a new family during the last several months. Without your kindness, my girls and I never would have made it. I think it's fitting we marry and begin this new journey together, don't you?"

"Um…"

Sliding her arm through the crook at his elbow, she surprised him by scooting closer to him on the seat before adding, "I feel we'll make a fine family and we should tackle this wilderness as one."

Trying to keep himself from wiggling like a puppy, Willis brushed a kiss across her cheek and said, "Thank you, Elizabeth."

"You're welcome."

"I'm not sure Fort Hall will have a preacher, though," he added.

"We'll find one."

Topping a ridge, the settlers fanned out and reined up their teams to bask in the scene below. The Snake River meandered gently and sparkled in the sunlight. On the other side stood Fort Hall. Nestled behind log and adobe walls, it had become a fixture for settlers bound for the Oregon Territory.

The air seemed to exhale as a long collective sigh went up from the travelers. All their trials, heartache and tribulations seemed to vanish as they gazed upon their destination. Soon the families would separate and move onto their new homes and lives, forever carrying the memories of their long journey. They would retell the adventures by fireside for years to come.

The men who were responsible for guiding them sat their mounts quietly. They, too, were happy to see the fort in the distance. It meant their journey's end was near and the wagon train they had guided was mostly intact. They all were proud of the accomplishment, although no one spoke of it.

As usual, Packy interrupted all their thoughts. "Well, there it be," he remarked.

"Yup."

"Don't seem possible we was able to wrangle these greenhorns and get them here after all these months."

"Nope."

"You still got that itch between your shoulder blades, James?" Micah asked

The French-Canadian jostled his shoulders and replied, "Nope."

"This bunch'll be as happy as a passel of skunks under their covers tonight, ya?" said the Swede.

Micah chuckled and agreed, "Reckon so."

"Guess, I can uncross my fingers now, huh?" Packy added.

"Yeppers."

The four maintain men rested for a few days before deciding to head back home. As they cut their pack mules from the remuda and prepared to depart, the settlers surrounded them. One and all wanted to say goodbye and thank them for leading the train to new and promising pastures.

After pumping the hands of the woodsmen, Thigpen said, "Thank you just doesn't seem to be enough for what you all did for us. Please, know we are forever grateful."

Elizabeth stepped forward and added, "If you are ever

this way again, come find us. You are always welcome at our fire." She slid her arm around Willis' waist and smiled with gratitude.

"We might just do that, ma'am," Micah said.

"Mr. Cunningham, thanks for teaching me all that stuff," JP said.

"You are welcome, son," he replied, ruffling the lad's hair and smiling.

Many of the settlers shed tears as they watched their heroes cross the Snake and head east.

"Now, we gonna go hunt some buffs?" asked Packy.

"Might be too late," teased James.

"Naw, it ain't," Packy added.

"Mushy Drummond, the freighter, probably already come and gone."

Packy frowned, reined his mule to a stop and asked, "What month is it anyways?"

The rest didn't stop to answer their talkative sidekick; they were too eager to head east. It was James yelled over his shoulder and said, "Time to hunt buffs, Packy!"

"About time!" he said and kicked his mule into a trot so he could catch up with the others.

THE END

Thank you for reading **Hell on Wheels.** *I hope you*

enjoyed it as much as I enjoyed creating it.

Please leave a review of my work at Amazon or any of the social networking sites that provide promotional venues for authors.

In the meantime, enjoy a sneak peek from **Miss Birgit's Dilemma,** *book #2 in the Oregon Trail series and the continuing adventures of Micah, Johan, James and Packy continues.*

ABOUT THE AUTHOR

Author Juliette Douglas pets Artic Bright View, the thoroughbred stallion that played "Silver" in the 2013 remake of The Lone Ranger. Both hail from Marshall County, Kentucky (Photo by Lois Cunningham, Benton, KY)

Juliette Douglas is a two-time Laramie Award winner for her novels, "Copperhead," and "Bed of Conspiracy." She is an independent author who has more than one dozen titles to her credit.

"King" is her first release of 2022 and will be followed by "Moon Pies & Moonshine" later this year.

Douglas is Kentucky's Wild West tale-spinner. Her novels are packed with spirit, suspense, heart and romance. Her fast-paced, hard-hitting stories about strong, bold and brassy women in the Old West are a winning combination for her readers. Men, women and teens alike enjoy traveling back in time, eating dust, shivering in the cold, sitting around a campfire and telling tales or riding the trail with her characters. She paints a vivid palette of landscape, hard times, true friends, quirky characters and happy endings.

She is a rescue Mom with two dogs, two cats and two possums, who were featured in her first children's book, "We Are Awesome Possums." She plans to add more tales about awesome critters in the future.

You can find her on a variety of social media sites, including Amazon, Facebook, Goodreads, Twitter and Cowboy Kisses.

All you have to do is: "Saddle up and ride!"

EMAIL AUTHOR

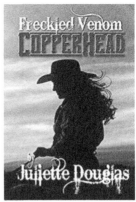

Juliette Douglas is a two-time winner of the prestigious Laramie Award for Western Fiction.

KING IS A HIT

Amazon readers love it.

"I enjoyed this story of loss, survival and regaining reasons to keep learning to live while dealing with catastrophe, attacks by pirates and scammers. A sweet ending."

"Characters that grab the storyline and take it where they wish to head. Well thought out. Stole my afternoon from me. Started out to just fill time and here it is well past my bedtime. I await the next work in progress from this excellent storyteller. Write faster."

"This book is written so finely, I could not find fault. I cried and I laughed. Separation from the ones you love is not joke and Juliette Douglas has captured tragedy and love once again in her latest novel. Please take the time to enjoy this book. I think you will find that you will want to read on and explore somewhere new. Rex is a hero in my book. Don't you want to find out how? I challenge anyone not to like this book."

THE DOUGLAS COLLECTION

Freckled Venom Series
Copperhead
Copperhead Strikes
Skeletons
Vixen
Oregon Trails Series
Hell on Wheels
Miss Birgit's Dilemma
Other titles
Plum Dickens of a Christmas
Pocketful of Stars
The Littlest Cowboy
Mistletoe & Horseshoes
Bed of Conspiracy
Perfume, Powder & Lead: Holy Sisters
We Are Awesome Possums

VISIT AMAZON

ACCLAIM FOR DOUGLAS

Juliette Douglas is a multi-award-winning author who has twice earned the prestigious Laramie Award for Western Writing, the most recent in 2020 for Bed of Conspiracy.

COPPERHEAD

"I have read several of her books and I am fortunate to live in western Kentucky and have met her. I love and highly recommend her books. If you're looking for good reads, she's the author you're looking for. Truly, as she says when she signs my books, enjoy the ride."

"This book is written with deep understanding of people and a perception of both the good and the evil of the human heart."

"Female protagonist and female author will both speak to the hearts of men and women who love the Old West."

"I find Juliette Douglas' approach to be formulaic, as in a formula that works. Simple effective, fun and engrossing"

"I really enjoyed reading the 1st two books and can't wait for the 3rd…I have to be honest; I wasn't expecting a very good western from a woman author...you changed my mind!"

POCKETFUL OF STARS

"Juliette Douglas has written another great read! Filled with family, love, friendship & action. Don't want to give any spoilers away, so read it. You won't be disappointed. Thumbs up!"

WE ARE AWESOME POSSUMS

"My granddaughter loves this book. She holds a stuffed possum while her momma reads it."

"Most authors do not transition very well from their regular genre to writing a children's book. You knocked it out of the ballpark on your first try with your book, Awesome Possums."

"I was drawn to this book for two reasons: 1-I also write children's books and 2-I love possums."

"Awesome Possums should be on your "read" list. The author, Juliette Douglas and illustrator Steven Barton have published this funny, yet educational book about a family of "rescue" possums. Brothers Jake and Jasper take us on a journey about life as rescued possums in a household of siblings, a kitten and "monster dog" named Scout. They tell us some interesting possum facts as well as funny possum observations. This is a good read along book for parents and teachers as some of the words used (and explained) may be difficult for a child to read alone the first time."

"The story is great! The illustrations are funny and creative."

"Highly recommended!

SNEAK PEEK

MISS BIRGIT'S DILEMMA
Mail order Bride

By

JULIETTE DOUGLAS

Traveling to the heart of the majestic Rocky Mountains, mail order bride Birgit Andersson doesn't know what to expect when she arrives in Sinking Springs to meet her prospective husband, Johan Svenson. Will God step in and provide direction amidst the sprawling wilderness that is home to a few brave men and fewer courageous women?

Chapter One

Spring 1857

Three teams of mules pulled the heavily laden freight wagon along a spindly, muddy stretch of road that was hardly a road at all. Sometimes it was lined with a brace of granite escarpment on one side and nothing on the other, scaring Birgit Andersson half to death as she stared down the bottomless pit to her left. Other times they traveled through thick forest growth, the fresh scent of spruce and pine tickling her senses.

Mushy Drummond glanced furtively at his pale dark blonde passenger.

She's a game one to be traveling by herself.

He remembered how she had approached him at Mountain Valley stage depot and way station and asked if he knew where Sinking Springs was and if he knew a man named Herr Johan Svenson. Well, that was that. He'd known Johan for years.

She'd proved her mettle by taking over his cooking duties as they traveled farther into the mountains. She was a fine cook, too. He enjoyed the meals the woman put together with game Drummond killed along the trail.

Birgit no longer felt excited with the anticipation of beginning a new life. Traveling by train, then by stagecoach and now freight wagon, she just wanted to get to her new home. A Swedish mail order bride from Scandia, Minnesota, she was traveling to the heart of the western frontier, the Rocky Mountains. She had no idea what awaited her.

"Miss, not much longer now," the driver said. "Maybe another day and a half 'fore we get ta Sinking Springs." He glanced sideways at the young woman sitting tiredly on the bench seat. "I knows this has been hard on ya, but I kin see ye are a stout one and a beauty at that."

Blushing at the driver's comments, she answered in her soft Swedish accent, "Thank you, Herr Drummond. That was kind of you."

She never thought of herself as pretty. There were far more beautiful women back home. Birgit didn't have the flaxen hair or the fair complexion like other Swedish maidens, making her feel like an outcast amongst her own people. She was older than most, too, well beyond the age most women married.

"Ya be leaving family behind?" Drummond questioned.

"No, no family," Birgit said, giving him a faint smile. Her mind wove through old memories of when another Swedish family had invited her to travel to America. Her heart had yearned for adventure and excitement; she wanted to see what this new America was like. Taking them up on their offer, she said goodbye to her parents, brothers and sisters.

Her thoughts of home made her sigh longingly.

Has it really been ten years since I left Sweden?

She shook her head in disbelief as she moved around on the hard bench seat, trying to make herself more comfortable. It was no use; the wood still felt like she was sitting on a rock.

"Johan Svenson is a good man. Gets a might rowdy at times but a good man ta have on yer side if'n there's trouble."

Birgit just nodded.

She had spent the last ten years of her life as a handmaiden to a local family in Scandia, eventually paying back the cost of her fare to Americas. Afterward, she saved every penny she could. When Birgit felt she had enough, she took the plunge and began scouring ads in the local Swedish papers, dreaming of becoming a mail order bride. Of course, deep down, it was love and happiness for which she yearned.

When she found an advert from a Swede, who, like herself, was seeking companionship. She wrote to him and waited for a response. After months, she had given up hope of ever receiving a reply. She decided to check the postal boxes at the mercantile one last time and, lo and behold, a message was inside.

A small gasp escaped her lips and grey eyes grew round staring at a battered rectangular package, wrapped in oilpaper and a thin strip of leather. Her heart fluttered uncontrollably. Her hand shook as her fingers reached, hesitated a moment and finally plucked the dingy, stained package from the cubbyhole. Looking over her shoulder to see if anyone was watching, Birgit tucked it deep within the folds of her cloak and quickly exited the mercantile.

Outside her feet moved quickly until she was running to her favorite place in town, the livery. Pulling a side door open, she entered and leaned against the door to catch her breath. The pungent warm smells of the stable calmed her nerves ever so slightly. When she had somewhat gathered her wits about her, Birgit scurried to the loft ladder, gathering her skirts as she nimbly climbed the steps. Only when she had settled down in the fragrant hay did she pull the package out. Her hands gently caressed the oilpaper as something precious, fingering the odd leather tie instead of string.

Her heart thumped hard within her chest, making it difficult to catch her breath as Birgit slipped the leather off the package. The oilpaper crackled as she opened it. Inside, she found a neatly folded letter with a return address of General Delivery, Sinking Springs, Colorado.

As she unfolded it, paper currency fell into her lap. She gasped and stared blankly at the bills, which amounted to forty dollars! It had taken her years to save forty dollars. Now, she held the money against her breast as if it was a prized family heirloom and smiled.

She placed the money in her lap, settled deeper into the hay and began reading the letter from Johan Svenson.

Miss Andersson,

Someone is writing this for me, the same way he wrote the ads for the periodical.

I ain't much on reading and writing. I been a mountain man far too long. Don't know much else, except I can provide a good home for you, and I'd be proud if you would be my wife.

Johan Svenson,

X — My mark

Birgit was astounded by the brevity of the note.

That's it?

She looked on the front and back to make sure she didn't miss something. Then, she reread the neat script and smiled. Flopping back in the hay, she gave a huge sigh. Then, doubt kicked in and caused her to abruptly sit up.

What have I done? He can't read or write? Should I travel west to marry a heathen, even though he said he could provide a good home for me. What kind of home, a cave or a pit dug into the earth with canvas for a ceiling?

Her mind conjured up all kinds of scenarios, causing her breathing to become short and shallow. She flopped back against the hay and closed her eyes, willing herself to calm down. Her insides felt as if she were churning buttermilk.

Of her many thoughts, a devilish one worried her most.

I could just keep the money and not go!

"Don't be silly," she whispered to herself. "Johan sent the money in good faith, trusting you would come and be his wife. For months this is the message for which you have prayed."

Sighing deeply, Birgit rose, shook and brushed her cloak to rid it of remnants of hay. Straightening her shoulders, she marched the few paces to the ladder and began her descended to the dirt floor. Then, Birgit Andersson strode purposely to the side door and slid through.

She was determined to make the best of her situation. She promptly packed what few belongings she had, bought her ticket and finally began her journey west into the unknown. She was determined to become Johan Svenson's bride.

Chapter Two

Sawing on the reins, Drummond slowed the triple team to a trot and guided them to a stop in front of one of the few buildings in the settlement of Sinking Springs. Wrapping the lines around the brake, Drummond stepped down. Looking at his passenger, he drawled, "Be right back, Miss. Gonna go find some boys to begin unloading." He walked around the rear of the wagon into the store.

Heaving a huge sigh of relief, Birgit let her gaze roam over her new surroundings. The mountains presented a feeling of closeness, nestling the little settlement within its hollow. Her eyes flowed upward following the mountain ridge with its granite peaks and dark green coat of pines and evergreens. New-growth leaves tinted the lower elevations with spring like color. She breathed deeply of the crisp air. It was so unlike where she had come from.

The air back home is nothing like this...

She stopped at mid-thought because she didn't care to look back; she was looking forward.

No. this is home now.

The freight driver charged out of Trader Charley's Post and said, "C'mon, Miss. This here is your stop."

He reached his hands up to guide her down from the high wagon seat. Settling her firmly on solid ground, he climbed aboard and retrieved the small, worn carpetbag that held her belongings.

Taking her elbow, Drummond led her toward the steps and a wooden bench outside the store. Handing the bag to her, he cleared his throat and asked "Um… Miss, did Johan know you were coming?"

Before answering, Birgit looked down at her hands. They gripped the worn handles of the bag so tightly her knuckles were white; She shook her head and said, "No, I don't believe so. I left as soon as I received his letter of invite."

Drummond resettled his hat on his head, pursed his lips and blew out some air before saying, "Well then. Have ta send someone up to his place and let him know you're here."

He turned to go back to his freight wagon, but Birgit stopped him, touching his arm ever so slightly. Drummond paused to glanced back at the woman.

"What's does Johan do?" she asked.

"You don't know?"

Shaking her head, Birgit explained, "His letter didn't say. It was very short," she said with a smile.

"He's a mountain man, ma'am. Trapper. Hunter. Tracker. And a damn fine one at that!"

Blinking, Birgit tried to wrap her mind around the driver's words.

Oh, am I marrying a heathen?

She sighed inwardly and let out an uneasy breath of air.

Giving the woman a short glance, Drummond changed directions and entered the store again.

Grey eyes flicked over the small town, which consisted of three log buildings; the store where she sat and a livery with penned stock in a corral. The building farthest away had a crudely-painted sign above its entry, proclaiming it The Lucky Strike. The newcomer had no idea what kind of merchandise might be sold there.

Turning, she walked over to the fur pelts, tacked to the wall of the trading post. Reaching out, she cautiously touched one of the skins. Surprised at how soft and thick it was, her fingers wove their way into the softness, loving the luxurious feel against her hand. She continued to touch others, marveling at their softness.

↔

"Charley, that woman out there may need some lookin' after 'til we's can get Johan down here," Drummond explained, pointing to the female standing outside the trading post doors.

Trader Charley glanced at the woman and squinted at Drummond before saying, "Hell fire. Ya knows we ain't got no place to keep no woman!"

Glancing around, Mushy realized h Charley was right.

He turned back to the short and stout Irishman and said, "Just give her some blankets and put her in a corner 'til Johan comes."

Charley gave Drummond a squirrelly look.

"Where's yer squaw?"

"Got her out back working hides."

It was Mushy's turn to give Charley the squirrelly eye. "Well, this'un is a lady. She don't know nuthin' 'bout our kinda livin'. But she's a Swede like Johan. So, I reckon they'd be just fine together. He'll teach her our ways or she'll die learnin' 'em."

Chapter Three

Mesmerized by the furs, Birgit jumped when someone spoke softly in her ear. Turning, she blinked at the brazen closeness of a man in front of her. Her nose wrinkled as she caught scent of him.

"You be one mighty fine piece of womanhood," he said as he reached for her. His pungent and rancid taint came from one who bathes only on Christmas and Fourth of July, if then. Birgit held her breath as his odor swirled around her as she danced out of his way.

Birgit ran to her bag and held it up defensively in front of her as she whirled to face him. Her heart was thumping and her lungs felt like they were struggling for air. Birgit didn't know what she would do if he grabbed her.

Grey eyes continued to assess the man in front of her. He was not much taller than her, and his face was covered in a thick fur she suspected came from a winter of hibernation. She wondered what vermin lay under the beard, lice or flees. It was a disgusting thought.

Hazel eyes danced gleefully as he lewdly appraised the white woman. He stepped closer and said, "Aw, c'mon. I just want ta hold ya and smell that fine perfume ya be sportin'."

Birgit's bag came flying up, thumping him alongside the head. It surprised the hell out of the man, and he tumbled sideways into what passed for a street.

She blinked, not knowing where her response had come from. Birgit stared at her bag, then back at the man in the mud. She was struggling to breathe from exertion and fear.

Flying out the door in her defense, Drummond stopped at the edge of the walkway and chided the behemoth, "Randall, git your carcass outta here! This here is Johan Svenson's bride!"

Randall slowly rose, rubbed his head and stated, "Don't care. She ain't got no right to slug me."

Trader Charley came to stand behind the thickset Drummond.

"You want I should tell Svenson you accosted his bride?" the trader asked loudly.

Randall shook his head briskly, knowing full well the power behind one of Svensen's powerful punches.

"That's what I thought. She's done spoken for and had every right to slug you! Now, get along 'fore I take my turn 'fore Svenson arrives!"

"What's you sticking up fer her for?" Randall asked.

"This lady is my responsibility 'til Svenson comes and gets her. Now, you best hightail it!"

Walking toward The Lucky Strike, Randall glanced over his shoulder at the three of them standing in front of

Charley's place. Giving a shrug, he pushed open the door of the saloon.

He reckoned he needed a drink before he settled for his squaw, all smelling like bear grease instead of perfume. The thought didn't set too well with him after getting a whiff of a pretty white woman.

Breathing deeply, Birgit tried to calm herself. She had never been so scared in her life.

Drummond turned to her and asked, "You all right, Miss? He didn't hurt ya none, did he?"

Nodding slowly, she whispered, "I'm fine."

"Miss, this here is Trader Charley. He'll look after ya 'til Johan comes ta collect ya."

Surprised, Birgit finally managed to get the words out. "But... but... How long will that take?"

"A week, maybe less. Could be more, though."

Birgit gasped with dismay.

Thumbing over his shoulder, Drummond explained, "Johan lives way up in them there mountains, ma'am."

Birgit glanced in the direction the thumb was pointing then refocused on the burly freight driver.

"He got him a right purdy spot, too. But it's a ways off from here. He may be out checking his traplines or whatnot. So, it takes time to find him. Livin's hard here, ma'am, but there ain't no place on Mother Earth like it. Johan was excited to be gettin' a wife. So, he'll come lickety-split outta them mountains ta claim ya," Drummond explained and flashed a huge smile.

Standing a little taller, Birgit's nose shot upward and she stated firmly. "Herr Drummond, Johan Svenson will never claim me," she said indignantly.

Mushy and Trader Charley's eyes grew round.

"I intend to be his equal in every way," she continued. "I do not intend to be his mistress or his slave. I came all this way to be his wife and a fine wife I shall be."

That said, she turned smartly, still clutching the worn carpetbag and marched through the door of Trader Charley's establishment.

The brows of the two men cocked as they looked at each other with surprise. They wondered if their friend, Johan, knew what he was getting himself into.

END OF SNEAK PEEK

"Miss Birgit's Dilemma" was first published in 2017. Watch for this remastered version, which will be re-released this summer at Amazon.

SNEAK PEEK

KING

By

JULIETTE DOUGLAS

"The most terrifying face of death comes from the hands of those who just want to be left alone."

That was Rex King's philosophy after losing everything he held dear in the Great Chicago Fire of 1871. A teacher-turned-gambler, he plied his trade aboard the classic riverboats of the age.

King read his opponents with uncanny precision, caring only for the money he raked in. That was until a kindly captain and a stowaway crossed his path. Then, the stakes got much higher.

PROLOGUE

Chicago, October 8, 1871

"Fire! Fire!"

The word traveled quickly as the sound of water wagons, drawn by horse and mule and manned by a handful of trained fireman and scores of volunteers, raced to where a fire-breathing dragon was consuming everything in sight. The flames licked at the night sky as the inferno, which many say began in a barn, consumed a nearby home and then a neighborhood. It did not stop, though. It howled onward, sucking everything into a cavernous belly.

Screams of shock and horror became entangled with the roar of the unrestrained beast as it unleashed destruction faster than its humans could react.

Prayers went unheeded.

Hundreds of Chicagoans perished.

A six-week drought had compounded the situation, along with a mass of wooden structures with tar or shingle roofs, bone-dry boardwalks and alleyways filled with the debris of humankind. A strong southwest wind whipped and fueled the torrent into a raging cataclysm. The sheer heat of the firestorm ignited one parched building after another. The wind carried sparks of fury skyward and ignited new unmanageable fires a mile away.

Animals suffered alongside their owners. No one was safe from flying embers. There was nowhere to hide and few avenues of escape.

Those who fought against the fiery onslaught found themselves overcome by smoke and ash. Lungs surrendered long before the weary arms of bucket brigades gave out.

The dragon was unstoppable; it was consuming Chicago with each fiery breath.

CHAPTER 1

Outside light flickered and bounced off the interior wall of Marianne Fitzsimmons King's small flat. A muffled rising din of noise came from the street below and distracted her from reading to her four-year old daughter, Sara. She rose and placed the child with the book in a chair. When she opened the door and stepped outside, the commotion from the street below, was deafening.

Her chin dropped and her mouth made a silent "O" as she smelled the smoke, saw the flames raging two blocks away and scorching the night sky with ever increasing fury.

"My Lord! It's fire!" she gasped. Her hand flew to her neck and her concern immediately raced to her husband. "Rex, I've got to find him!" she whispered.

Instinctively, she spun and ran inside. She scooped up Sara and flew out the door, sprinting down three flights of stairs to the street. Chaos of the unmanageable greeted her eyes. Wearing only the clothes on her back as she sheltered her young daughter in her arms. Her eyes couldn't believe what she was witnessed at every turn. The fire was spreading quickly, too quickly. The air had become thick with smoke and heat as it raged ever closer.

Marianne sprinted north, knowing Rex was at one of the clubs, trying to supplement their meager teaching salaries. She entered the throng of refugees who fled the firestorm. At that moment she was glad that she had long legs.

Stopping to catch her breath, Marianne placed her shawl over Sara's head and face. Despite the panic that surrounded her, she spoke calmly to her daughter. "No matter what happens, do not let go of me. Do you understand?" she said.

Marianne felt the slight nod.

"Even if I fall, you hang on, all right?"

A breathless whisper answered, "Yes, Mama."

Marianne struggled to get her bearings in the madness surrounding her, but there was nothing but thick smoke and angry flames encircled them. Human and animal voices screamed in terror adding to the ear shattering sounds of the untamed beast.

She whirled, looking for an escape route. There was none.

Bile in her throat as she inhaled the ash-filled air. She tried to spit, but her mouth was too dry. Marianne felt the suffocation attack her body as if she were in a flame-filled tomb. She steeled herself against it.

"I'm not going to die!" she said under her breath. "We must find a way out! Then, we will find Rex!

With a new resolve and hugging Sara tighter, she tried to move away from the herd of jostling people. They seemed to be moving north into through a tunnel created by the arcing fire.

Marianne strained to find a way out but, at every turn,

heat and flames blocked her way. She felt the wind push the inferno one way, so she looked south and west and changed direction.

Jostled by the terrified crowd, she was knocked off her feet. She landed hard on her knees and grimaced.

"Mama?"

Giving a reassuring kiss to her daughter's cheek, Marianne whispered, "It's all right, Sara, just hang on."

She tightened her grip on the child, gathered her skirts, and pushed her way through the throng of people desperately trying to escape the fire-breathing dragon.

***

WHEN WORD OF the great fire reached the Waterfront Gentlemen's Club, where the men of Chicago gathered to gamble, all games of chance came to a screeching halt. Rex King, who frequented the club to supplement his meager teacher's salary, dropped his cards, gathered his money and ran. His family lived on the top floor of a three-flat walkup in the tenement section of the city. It wasn't great, but it was all they could afford.

He and his counterparts could see and smell the billowing smoke the minute they emerged from the posh establishment. It was obvious, this was no ordinary fire. A large portion of the city was burning. Rex took off running, praying he could reach his family before the flames did.

He ran recklessly through the streets, dodging the flames that seemed to spring up out of nowhere. The safety of his family was his only thought. The streets were packed with fleeing residents, animals and firefighting equipment. It was impossible to see if his wife and daughter were among the refugees. The smoke burned his throat and eyes. Tears left white streaks on his blackened cheeks. Still, he kept moving as fast as he could.

Heat and smoke seared his lungs, hot ashes singed his hair and flying embers burned holes in his clothing. His fingers were burned as he brushed away the molten enemy. The roar of the conflagration was deafening. Blinded by soot and smoke, he struggled onward, his lungs burning with each urgent stride.

When he finally reached what he thought was Ellsworth Street, there was nothing left of the line of tenements he once knew. Where they once stood were piles of charred debris and smoldering ashes. The heat was next to unbearable.

Frantically, he searched the clusters of people remaining. They were strangers with shocked, soot-covered faces. Their lives had been dismantled. Only dead eyes looked through him when he inquired about the whereabouts of his wife and daughter.

Numbly, he searched. Everything was black. All looked the same. He tried to regain his bearings. This couldn't have happened to the tenement he and his family shared. He had to be on the wrong street.

He turned in circles so he could gaze far and wide, but there was nothing to see. His neighborhood was gone. Normal landmarks no longer existed. The city continued to burn. He was alone in a scorched and smoldering world.

***

A SMOKY, GRAY hue enveloped the city as the sun rose on October 9, 1871. An acrid stench filled the air. Rex King could see the fire continued to rage on the western edges of town. Disheartened and depressed, he collapsed in a yard south of the fire zone. He assumed it was where children once played, perhaps one of his students.

"Mister! Hey, Mister! Are you all right?" a voice beckoned to him from afar. A firm hand pulled on the sleeve of his tattered and burned jacket.

As the fog lifted from his brain. King moaned, rolled over onto his back and tried to open his eyes. It was painful and agonizing. They felt swollen and they burned from the smoke he had stared into throughout most of the night.

"Mister?" the voice called again.

Then there was another voice. It was the voice of a female.

"Jimmy, you get away from that man!" his mother warned, stepping out of the house and marching toward him.

"But, Ma, he's hurt. Can't you see that?" answered ten-year old Jimmy.

"I don't care," she said and glanced to the west where the smoke still was billowing into the sky. "That fire is gonna send all kinds of riff-raft our way. Everyone will be looking for a handout. We ain't got nothing for them. Now, you come along."

Jimmy resisted.

"But Ma, he's hurt," he pleaded. "Can't we give him a glass of water?"

Struggling to stand, King finally made it to an upright position. His swollen eyes were tiny slits and his voice was hoarse when he spoke.

"If it's all right, I would like a glass of water," he begged. "It would be so kind if you have any to spare?"

She stared at him, taking account of his soot covered face, burned jacket and singed hair and eyebrows. He could barely stand.

"You may sit on the porch step. I'll bring you a glass of water," she agreed, taking her son's hand and pulling him toward the house. "Come along, Jimmy. The air is dreadful out here."

Hearing the front door slam, King moved to the step and sank down wearily. A few moments later he heard the door open and a hand lightly touch his shoulder.

"Here," the woman said.

Taking the glass, he nodded his thanks and gulped the tepid water. At first it burned going down, but it washed away the smoke and ash he had inhaled most of the night. He began to feel better.

She took the glass when he handed it to her and disappeared. When she returned with another full glass, he again was thankful.

"Much obliged, ma'am," he said.

Glancing toward the thick smoke, she asked, "How bad is it?"

He coughed hard, bringing up smoky mucus. He wanted to spit but it would be impolite. He swallowed and answered, "I don't know. I was with some friends when I heard the news. I rushed back to our home, where I hoped to find my wife and daughter. I couldn't even find our street."

His head dropped into his hands, and Rex struggled in vain to hold the moisture back that leaked from his swollen eyes. He coughed, hoping she wouldn't notice.

The woman saw the internal struggle going on within the stranger's body. She felt sorry for him.

Gathering his wits about him, King finished the water and wobbled to his feet, hanging onto a post for support. He handed her the glass and said, "Again, I'm much obliged for the water. I'll be going now."

As he walked back toward the ashen neighborhoods the dragon left in its path,, the woman suddenly felt sorry for him.

"I hope you find them," she called out as he resumed his search.

CHAPTER 2

Winding his way back north, Rex King stared numbly at the destruction. Hot spots still smoldered. Debris was everywhere. Men were digging in the rubble. Recovered bodies were being tossed into waiting wagons. He turned away quickly. As tears blurred his vision, King stumbled into the path of another wagon.

The driver yelled as he sawed on the reins, "Hey! Get outta the road, ya drunken sot!"

The voice alerted King of the oncoming danger. He rolled out of the way, barely dodging the hooves of a team of horses as the wagon lumbered past. Rising slowly, he gazed at the broken, mangled and charred bodies thrown haphazardly into the wagon's bed. He took a deep breath that burned his lungs and made him cough. This time he expelled the cloudy mucus. He prayed his wife and daughter were not among the bodies being carted off.

King plodded on; wreckage crunching underfoot. He had no idea where he was. All the familiar landmarks were gone. Spying a pair of Chicago policemen, he slogged over to them.

They watched as he approached sorrowfully. They had seen many men just like Rex King wandering the streets in search of loved ones.

"Officers? I wonder if you could help me?" he asked.

They remained silent and waiting. Tired bloodshot eyes looked out from their own ash covered and grim faces. The fire had taken its toll, too, on the men charged to keep the peace in such catastrophic times.

"Um, my name is Rex King and I'm trying to locate my wife and daughter," he said as he pointed to where he guessed his home once stood. "We used to live down there somewhere in the tenement section."

The pair threw a quick glance at each other and then back to King. One answered. "A temporary morgue has been set up at the livery at 64 Milwaukee Avenue." an officer said flatly.

The answer slammed King in the gut and extinguished his breath. He wasn't giving up. He took a deep gulp of air and asked, "What about the survivors? Where would they be?"

"They would be at the First Congregational Church on Washington Street," the second officer informed. "All facilities west of the fire have been instructed to provide relief and rescue stations for survivors."

"Thank you. Thank you very much," Rex replied, quickly backing away.

The officers shook their heads as the watched him trudge off. They saw no hope in his staggered gait.

***

ARRIVING ON Washington Street, King was shocked at the amount of people seeking refuge. Long lines of fire survivors wound down the street and around the corner. Hope rose in his heart.

If there are this many survivors, I'm certain to find Marianne and Sara here.

Picking up his pace, he frantically searched for a tall slender brunette and a little girl as he examined the lines of people seeking relief. Not seeing any familiar figures, he pushed his way through the waiting refugees and climbed the steps to the church nimbly. He was excited. He was confident his family inside would be inside.

A cacophony of noise hit him as he entered the makeshift refuge. Babies cried. Voices were raised in fear and anger. Children screamed, still terrified by the fiery ordeal and the loss of comfort. Again, he became overwhelmed by the sights and sounds but remained committed to finding his family. This is where his wife and daughter would be found. Refocusing on the task, he turned to his left and approached the first station.

Unable to gain anyone's attention, King plowed around a table but was stopped by a police officer. Rex starred him down. With urgency in his voice, he proclaimed, "I'm looking for my wife and daughter."

"Get back in line!" the officer stated firmly.

King would not be deterred, "Do you have a written record of who all is here?" he asked.

The officer nodded toward a pile of papers at the edge of the table.

Seeing that, King began scouring the list of hurriedly scrawled names. Once his heart took a leap when he saw the name Marianne, but it faded quickly when the last name did not match his own. Frantically, he continued flipping page after page but didn't find his surname anywhere. Fear rose in his chest, threatening to cut off his air flow again. He laid the papers down, glanced around the room and marched to the next table. The process continued until all the pages had been read at each station.

The teacher's shoulders slumped in defeat. He managed to find a vacant piece of wall to lean against and closed his eyes, trying to quell the feeling of doom he felt.

I'm not giving up! I'll find them!

With renewed resolve, Rex opened his eyes and scanned the room. Brown eyes flittered from face to face. They stopped and zeroed in on the back of a slender woman tending to a small girl.

Marianne!

His heart swelled as he pushed his way through the throng. When he got close, he called her name, "Marianne!"

The woman turned at the sound of his voice.

Immediately, King's charge came to a halt. She wasn't his wife after all.

"I'm sorry, ma'am," he apologized. "I thought you were someone else."

She nodded and turned back to the little girl.

King retreated, the soles of his shoes dragging against the planked floor.

He spent the rest of the day visiting every relief and rescue station set up for fire victims. The result was the same.

Distraught, he made his way to the waterfront. He limply slid onto the ash-covered sands. Despair gripped his heart as he listened to the waves slap against the shore. They lulled him into an exhausted sleep.

***

THE MORNING OF October 10 was no different than the day before. Chicago continued to burn. Fueled by the easy fodder of sunbaked, wooden structures and boardwalks, the fire-breathing dragon gobbled up every piece of dried pine, oak and elm in its path. It raged westward with total destruction in mind.

King awoke to lead-colored skies that added to his misery. His breathing was difficult, and his chest hurt. His eyes burned. Without warning, he convulsed, coughing up the gray mucus that clogged his lungs. He flopped back against the sand, his chest and abdomen aching from his fitful effort to expel the smoke from his system.

The fresh Lake Michigan air provided him with renewed resolve. He had one more place to check -- the livery at 64

Milwaukee Avenue. It had been turned into a makeshift morgue. He closed his eyes and rested his head on his sandy knees. He dreaded going there, but he had no choice. He had to know what happened to Marianne and Sara.

***

KING COULDN'T believe his eyes as he stood at the open double doors of the livery. Rows of charred bodies were strewn everywhere. There was barely room to walk among them.

"You lookin' for someone?" asked the guard.

He answered with a nod that was barely perceptible, the shock too great to speak. Finally, King cleared his throat and muttered, "My wife and daughter."

"I see."

"Have you identified the victims?"

"Can't. All we could do was put toe tags on them, indicating the location from where they were found." He pointed at the scores of bodies that filled the main concourse of the livery and added. "There's some in the stalls, too."

King closed his eyes. His head was spinning so rapidly it was making him sway from exhaustion, lack of food and water.

The guard steadied him and guided him to an exterior wall to keep him from toppling over. As soon as his back found support, he slid to the ground and closed his eyes.

"You just rest here for a bit. I'll get you some water," the officer said. He returned with a canteen and passed it to the suffering stranger.

King unscrewed the top and guzzled the refreshing water. While wiping his mouth with a grungy sleeve, he returned the canteen to the guard and said, "Much obliged."

Nodding, the officer asked, "What part of town you from?"

"Ellsworth. But it's not there anymore."

The guard winced. "That's near DeKova, where the damn fire started."

"And it's still burning," King said, making more of a statement than a question.

Taking a deep breath, he pushed himself to a standing position. With one hand pressed against the wall for stability, King inched forward toward the collection of cadavers. He steeled himself against the thought of finding Marianne and Sara with toe tags. He stumbled through the opening, forcing himself to examine every grotesque face. Eyes stared into eternity. Mouths hung open in silent torment.

At the farthest end of the livery, he found corpses with toe tags that indicated the remains were found near Ellsworth Street. All the bodies were adult forms. There were no children. He glanced into a stall filled with more charred remains. Smaller bodies were laid next to larger frames. He examined the toe tags. None were from Ellsworth.

King continued until he had examined every one of the dragon's victims. Exiting, he again leaned against the exterior wall and tried to hold back tears. With his raspy voice, he had to ask one more question of the guard.

"Are there any other morgues set up?"

"Nope. This is the only one so far. But the damn fire is still burning. There will be more."

Nodding King trudged away, heading to the waterfront. He didn't know what else to do. He had nowhere else to go.

When he got there, he again sat in the sand to ponder what to do next. His heart told him their tenement was too close to the origin of the fire. He had to accept the fact Marianne and Sara had perished.

The world he once cherished was gone. He laid bare his anguished soul on the shores of the great lake. This was the day his Chicago died. Then, without warning, the rains came. Torrents of water from the skies mingled with Rex King's salty tears. They helped wash away the past and gave birth to a new beginning.

END OF SNEAK PEEK

"King" *was published in 2022 and has gotten rave reviews from readers. It is available exclusively at Amazon.*

Made in the USA
Monee, IL
20 October 2023

44927300R00148